A SINGLE BREATH

AMANDA APTHORPE

Copyright (C) 2021 Amanda Apthorpe

Layout design and Copyright (C) 2021 by Next Chapter

Published 2021 by Next Chapter

Edited by Terry Hughes

Cover art by CoverMint

Dedicated to my parents, Sid and June Jones,
and my sister, Andrea Madeline Jones

I had become only too aware that life's beginning and its end hinged on a single breath, as though the rest was conducted in its pause.

CHAPTER ONE

MELBOURNE, AUSTRALIA

The ceiling of the cabin sagged so low that I could measure its distance to my face with a wide-fingered handspan. A cold light from the bathroom cubicle ricocheted around the walls and reflected off the panels above my nose. Where they met, someone had picked at the seam like a child at a scab. With each pitch and toss of the ferry, diesel fumes seeped through its pores.

There was no sound from the bunk below. My sister, I assumed, was sleeping peacefully, but I needed the comfort of her enthusiasm. In the space left to me, I contorted my body so that my head and torso hung over the bunk's edge.

"Madeleine. Are you awake?"

There was a low groan and the sound of the bunk springs creaking as she rolled over.

"What?" Her yawn was thick with sleep.

"What are we doing here Mads?"

No reply, just a soft snore at the back of her throat. I rolled back to stare again at the ceiling's ragged seam. A dog barked in a cabin somewhere further along the deck.

In the darkness of what I feared would be our watery crypt, I doubted the wisdom of this journey.

CHAPTER TWO

It had begun with the arrival of the first letter. What I remember about that day is tinted with soft shades of autumn. It must have been warm because I was sitting in my courtyard reading the newspaper. I looked up, drawn by a tone in Madeleine's voice.

The air seemed to shimmer around her strong and solid body as she moved towards me. My own depleted frame would have cut that air like a dulled blade. Her arm was raised as if she was about to slap the letter, she held on to the cast iron table and her face was pinched with familiar concern. When I took it from her, I saw that my name and address were written in Indian ink in an old-fashioned hand. She sat as I broke the seal. Inside was a sheet of parchment paper folded over. As I opened it, a small stone rattled on to the table.

"What does it say?" Madeleine nodded towards the note and shuffled closer in the protective way she had adopted in those months. She picked up the stone and rolled it in her fingers.

The letters of a foreign language were written in the centre of the page.

"It's not in English," I said and passed it to her. She tried to sound what looked to be three words and shrugged as she handed it back. I studied it more closely.

"It could be Greek." The envelope was face up and I took in the postmark. "It's been sent from Kos," I said.

"Where?"

"A Greek island near the Turkish coast."

My sister's eyes shone in response. She was always eager for mystery, a trait that had led her into more daring adventures than I would ever contemplate. I picked up the stone and held it in one hand beneath the table. I returned to reading the newspaper, feigning a lack of interest in the letter but in truth I felt a small, quiet dread.

"What do you make of it, Dee?"

I looked up and met her eyes. "It's probably another hate letter."

She picked up the envelope and seemed to be measuring the weight of the words with a small movement of her hand.

"I don't think so," she said. "It's different from the others. Why be cryptic about hating someone?"

"Well, don't read too much into it," I said, flicking over a page of the paper with a finality that drew on my status as her older sister. The palm of my hand throbbed around the stone.

That night I woke at 2.20. My mother had once told me that it was the hour that people are most likely to die. I had believed her, but in all my years of medical practice had not seen any evidence, though my work was normally concerned with life's fragile start.

In more recent times, I had become only too aware that life's beginning and its end hinged on a single breath, as though the rest was conducted in its pause.

It was another dream that had woken me and the memory of it continued to resonate. For a while, I lay beneath the covers, allowing it to filter through.

There stands a man, his hand outstretched to me. Snakes writhe at his feet as they slide from a narrow pink vein embedded in a marble pedestal. I watch in fascination, then in horror, as I realise that it is not marble, but the body of a lifeless woman. The pink veins become blue. I turn at the feel of another's breath and see a woman, her hair braided. "Who are you?" I ask. She is about to speak her name...

By 3.30, I'd poured my third cup of tea. If I were Madeleine, it would have been peanut butter eaten by the spoonful to relieve anxiety. I wanted to call her but resisted. Aside from the late hour, I couldn't bear her analysis of the dream and suspected that I already knew some of what she would say – the snake was my kundalini energy finally releasing. We thought differently, but what kept me at the table, breathing long draughts of tea-steam through my nostrils, was that Madeleine and I would agree on the significance of the dead woman.

At 4am, a two-week-old newspaper that I had saved was spread before me. I knew what was in there but had never opened it until that moment. At page five, I saw the small article, the shards of my life collected into 100 or so words. The gist of it read: *Verdict not guilty; professional integrity restored; the plaintiff, struggling to reconcile the birth of his daughter and the death of his wife; the wife... dead from unforeseen causes.*

I reread the article and said the wife's name aloud – Bonnie – like an incantation. I wished that she hadn't had a name so that it might hurt less.

Exonerated of all blame – did all she could... But the words didn't provide me with any comfort.

"It wasn't your fault!" Madeleine had said and her expression had been desperate with the fear that I could have a breakdown.

How is a person meant to come to terms with being implicated in the death of another?

Leaning on my old oak dining table, a favourite of the "glory box" I abandoned when Julian left, I got up, physically and mentally aching, and went to the bookshelf. A well-meaning friend had suggested that I record my thoughts after Bonnie's death as a kind of therapy. I followed her advice, looking for anything that would ease the pain of it and the case brought against me by Bonnie's husband.

I took the envelope that had arrived that day from my pocket. The stone dropped into my hand as I looked at the note. Although I couldn't understand them, the words made me uneasy. I slipped it between the pages of the diary. From the drawer of the desk, I took out my jewellery box. Apart from a string of pearls and a jade scarab beetle, a souvenir from Madeleine's trip to Egypt, there was little else inside. Before the stone joined them, I studied it as it lay in my palm. It was no more than two millimetres thick, but it felt cold in the warmth of my hand. It was either marble or quartz and had a thin, rust-red vein that made it blush.

At 5am and feeling soothed, whether by the tea or exhaustion, I climbed back into bed. I slept then, a dreamless sleep and longer than I'd slept for months. When I awoke, I lay beneath the covers as I had done so many mornings since Bonnie's death.

Refreshed, I grew restless quickly and felt a return of an old eagerness to begin the day. I showered with a sense of purpose and felt a craving for a coffee and croissant in Chapel Street – I hadn't done that in a long time. The gate's click sounded a note of approval as it closed behind me.

At my regular café, I bypassed the pavement tables; the cooling autumn weather was beginning to creep into my toes. From a seat by the window, I looked out, regretting that I had missed the sun's warmth and the hot, lazy days that had come and gone that summer when I'd barely left the house.

Deb came to take my order and smiled. "Haven't seen you for a while, Dana. Been away?"

"Yes," I lied but didn't offer any more. She didn't ask.

"Lucky you. I could do with a break... maybe the Greek Islands," she whispered close to my ear before she left to seat a couple who had just walked in.

Before long, I found myself in the travel section of a local bookshop looking for a practical guide to Greece. The little I knew about Kos had come from my fruiterer, Kym, who would become misty-eyed when he'd spoken of the home he'd left 20 years earlier. From his description, it sounded beautiful, as home does when you're far away and feeling nostalgic.

There was nothing specifically about Kos, but I thumbed through the contents of a Lonely Planet guide and found it. "... third-largest island of the Dodecanese... five kilometres from the Turkish Peninsula of Bodrum..." I scanned its history. "Hippocrates, the father of medicine, was born and lived on the island." Hippocrates.

There was a small grip of pain in my solar plexus that I could no longer distinguish as physical or emotional. I recalled how proud and emotional I had been when I swore his famous oath, and in particular the line: "I will follow that system of regimen, which, according to my ability and judgement I consider for the benefit of my patients and abstain from whatever is deleterious and mischievous. I will give not deadly medicine..."

Bonnie's stricken and pleading face swam in front of me, and I felt again the shock of the first hate letter that arrived in the days after her death: "EVIL. MURDERER."

CHAPTER THREE

M adeleine's snore caught in the back of her throat, and I
heard the springs groan as she sat up suddenly.

"Are you awake, Dee?"

"Yes."

"Have you slept?"

"No."

"Me neither."

My eyes rolled to the ceiling. "Mads, I've been thinking..."

"Yes?" Her voice sounded guarded.

"That we've made a big mistake."

There was silence from below. An expert now at contorting
in small spaces, I leaned down, inverting my head towards her.
"Mads?"

"Why, Dee? Because the sea's a bit rough?"

"A bit rough! No, it's not that, it's just... the whole thing is...
crazy. Why are we here?"

"No, it's not crazy. We're meant to come."

"Really. Please don't tell me: 'It's our destiny.'"

"But it is."

I leaned further over the bunk's rail, "Oh Mads, come off it. Based on what? A letter we don't understand. A small piece of marble that could be a chip off a headstone – a warning!"

Silence again, then the creaking springs as she got out of bed. She staggered to the bathroom trying to maintain her balance as the boat lurched sideways. As she shut the door, I was left in the darkness. I flipped on my back, feeling guilty that I was all but blaming my sister. After all, I was the one who had organised this trip.

Outside the bookshop, I had paused to consider my next move and stepped aside to allow a mother with a baby in a pram to pass me on the narrow footpath. Tucking the Lonely Planet guide under one arm, I walked behind them, trying to prevent my thoughts from taking their familiar diversion into bleakness. Instead, the bright fluorescent lights of a travel agency drew me in and a friendly glance invited me to the counter. A young woman whose name tag read Karen finished tapping at the keyboard and swivelled to give me her attention.

"I'm thinking of going to Greece," I said.

"Return?"

And then, surprising myself again, I answered: "One way."

When I told Madeleine what I had done, her reaction caught me by surprise.

"You're leaving next Friday!" she said, unable to disguise the disappointment in her voice. She had been my constant companion in the preceding months, almost my carer.

"But you're the one who suggested I go," I reminded her.

"Yes..." Madeleine studied her fingernails.

"Oh, and by the way..." I tapped the table and spoke to her hands. "If you can arrange the time, there's a ticket on hold for you, too."

"Are you kidding?"

I smiled at the memory of that moment.

"No, I'm not kidding," I said and touched her fingers. "I just want to thank you. You've been really great, Mads, and I don't know what I would have done without you."

"You're my sister." Her eyes looked dangerously moist.

"So that's a yes?" I said, as I went into the kitchen. I took a deep breath as I filled the kettle.

"Mm, let me think..." Madeleine called across the kettle's hum. "If you insist."

"I do." I smiled into the two cups in my hand. "Your passport's still valid?"

Her head appeared around the kitchen doorway. "Yes... I've got to go."

"Where?" I asked.

"Home... to pack!"

In the bathroom cubicle, I could hear Madeleine cursing the paltry toilet flush. When she opened the door, the light was like the flash of a camera capturing my misery on the top bunk of a dying ferry.

She rummaged through her suitcase without speaking and returned to the bathroom, shutting off the light again in a clear statement of irritation. Blindly, I reached to the panels above my nose and gave them an equally irritated shove. My thoughts returned to the days before our departure. Although I had been putting it off, finally I made the telephone call I had been dreading.

"Dana... how are you?"

My eyes smarted at the sound of Ruth's voice. As chief of staff, she'd had a tough time during my court case. She'd never wavered in her support of me, despite the media's attempts to blacken the hospital's reputation. I had to compress my lips before replying.

"I'm well," I replied then came quickly to the point. "Ruth, I need time..."

Before I could finish, her soothing voice slid between us.

"Of course... I agree. How long would you like?"

I hesitated, the generosity and the security of what she was offering was tempting.

"I need to resign."

There was a sharp intake of air at the other end. "Dana, please reconsider. You could have six months... Take a year if you need it."

I paused, tempted. "I think it's the best thing, for me and for the hospital."

"I know what's best for this hospital, and you're a significant part of that."

"Thank you, Ruth. It means a lot to hear you say that. I'll never forget what you said in my defence."

"I've worked with you for 10 years. I meant every word of it."

"I've... lost the energy for it, Ruth, and the confidence, no doubt."

"That's to be expected, Dana. Give yourself some time."

"I am," I said with false conviction. "I don't know how long it will take, so it's best this way."

She was silent for a moment. "I'll accept your resignation, if you insist," she finally conceded. Her voice, always calm, was gentler still. "But there will be a place for you, if you change your mind. I'm just so sorry this ever happened to you. God bless, Dana."

As I said my goodbye, I wondered if I had acted too hastily and felt shaky with uncertainty. I was leaving my work, I was leaving my home, and I didn't really know why. I rang my parents. They were surprised to know that both their daughters would be away for an undetermined length of time.

"It'll be good for you, darling," my father said, and I felt the soothing balm of his love. He didn't question my decision to leave the hospital and I was grateful. My mother was less impressed.

"At least you'll be together."

I should have known that she would bring me little comfort.

CHAPTER FOUR

As I was packing, Madeleine arrived with travel gadgets – blow-up pillows, eye masks, drink bottles, lip salves that spilled across my dining room table.

"Freebies," she announced, "from one of my clients."

"No problem going away?"

"James can handle the business with his eyes closed."

Madeleine had built her landscape-design business to a level that she now employed staff.

"I'll probably become obsolete," she added.

"Hardly," I said, and meant it. My sister was the creative and business genius behind Gorgeous Gardens.

"So..." She arranged the items on the table distractedly. "I didn't ask you what you found out about Kos."

"Not much." I told her the little I knew.

She rifled through her handbag to produce a notebook that she waved at me.

"What's this?" I took it from her.

"The fruits of my own research."

I was surprised and she saw it on my face.

"Well," she said to my crooked eyebrow, "I didn't think you were up to it and..."

"You were." I laughed, grateful that my sister was predictably unpredictable.

The bathroom door opened. Madeleine paused, forming a striking silhouette in the door's frame. "Let's get out of here," she said, but I couldn't see her lips moving and the statement was strangely unsettling. Obediently, I slid from the bunk and dressed.

We took our chances with the unwelcoming crew and other passengers. The engines ground down and the ferry slowed its pace. From the windows of an almost-deserted lounge on an upper deck, we could see a smattering of island lights. The voice over the loudspeaker crackled that we were arriving at Kalymnos. Peering into the dark as the ferry went astern to dock, we could see an old fort tinted by amber lights brooding above the port. Only a dozen or so people disembarked and were swallowed by the night at the end of the pier.

"Not long now," I murmured, as much to myself as to Madeleine. She didn't answer.

A sigh of relief had escaped me when we'd finally boarded the plane to Greece. Farewells weren't my strong point, and I was irritated by my mother's sudden display of affection. On the way to Singapore, Madeleine was hyped. By the time we left for Athens, she'd burnt herself out. I shared her eagerness to leave Melbourne, and in fact my life, but at the same time it felt as though I was running away. I'd always taken pride in my ability to complete whatever I began and to go an extra step.

My father, though encouraging and proud of my achievements, would, in his most diplomatic way, suggest that I take things a little easier.

"You've achieved so much, Dana. What more do you need to do?"

I appreciated his concern, but I didn't feel that I could ever push myself too far. I thrived on the challenge of learning more, especially about my profession, and I thrived on success. Leaving felt like admitting defeat, and I wondered if I should have stayed to face my critics and resume my work. Somewhere along the way, though, I'd lost the inclination to do so.

On that long flight, my thoughts drifted to the day that changed my life, as they had for nearly every minute of every day for months. While Madeleine slept, I tried to steer them away, but the energy required was draining. Over and over, I had replayed the events of that day looking for something I might have missed – a sure sign of my guilt or, and I hated to admit it, someone else's – but there was nothing I could pinpoint, and the events had become distorted with time.

Everything about that day seemed to be wrong, even ominous, though it was a feeling born in retrospect. I'd had my own consultations and a delivery; I'd assisted two others, one a difficult birth and the other a seriously premature baby. After 14 hours without a break, I was tired. Just as I was getting ready to go home, Bonnie, one of my own patients, was rushed into Emergency with a profuse haemorrhage. Even though I was well used to the sight of blood, this time it shocked me and, for weeks afterwards, it ran as a stream of plasma with dark, malevolent clots that tinted my dreams.

I remember throwing aside my bag, raging with frustration when the rubber gloves curled in my palm as I hurriedly pulled them on, and I remember Bonnie's husband, grey with panic. Bonnie needed an emergency caesarean, but the anaesthetists were tied up with equally urgent cases. I had no choice but to administer the anaesthetic myself, but I couldn't place the tube in her throat. Bonnie's strangled gasps for air haunted my days afterwards.

From that point, my memory became blurred with time and shock. In the dreams that followed, I forced the tube deeper and deeper into her throat. In those dreams, Bonnie's eyes watched mine with unnerving attention, in others they pleaded with me to save her life. By all accounts, I acted swiftly and competently – that was the verdict, based on the testaments of those who had been present – but I wasn't convinced. Bonnie died from asphyxiation and her daughter was born soon after.

I leaned back into the seat, feeling the familiar despair rising in my chest. Deep-breathing techniques only pushed it further into my viscera. I fumbled for the bag I'd stowed beneath the seat and took out some of the material Madeleine had collected for research – two slim texts and some pages of notes she had jotted down from heavier volumes in the local library.

I opened one of the books, a treatise on a selection of the writings of Hippocrates and thumbed through its pages. The introductory section was academic and tedious, but the pages that followed were a collection of letters and speeches attributed to him.

On the left-hand-side of each double page, the text was written in Greek – Ancient Greek, I reasoned, and the English translation was written on the right. The early part, I read, was a plea from the people of Abdera to Hippocrates to heal their revered Democritus because they were afraid that he was going mad. But Hippocrates suspected that Democritus was showing the signs of attaining greater wisdom, the outward signs were being interpreted as madness. I wondered if my own outward signs over the past few months were consistent with some form of mental derangement.

I read on as Hippocrates recounted a dream: "I seemed to see Asklepios himself... snakes accompanied him. I turned and saw a large, beautiful woman with her hair braided simply... 'I beg you excellent one, who are you and what shall we call you?'"

I was stunned. Though a particular style of language was used, the woman in Hippocrates's dream resembled the one in my own. I reread the passage to convince myself that I was being fanciful, that I had latched on to one or two elements – the snake and the woman that could be represented in a million people's dreams.

The more I read it, the more profoundly it affected me. From the bag, I took out the letter from Kos and laid it on the tray in front of me. I ran my finger slowly down the Greek translation of Hippocrates' dream carefully comparing the Greek letters with those on the page of the note. In Letter 15, I identified them.

Madeleine stirred and opened her eyes, becoming alert at the sight of the letter and open book.

"Find something?"

"Mmm..." I steadied my breath. "Have a look at this."

I told her about my dream and what I'd found in the book. She sat up, excited, but not surprised. Nothing was a coincidence to my sister.

"Which parts of the dream do the Greek letters parallel?" she said, shifting in the seat.

I read aloud the preceding translation: "And what shall I call you?"

And there were the three words of the note: "'Truth,' she said."

My hand trembled and Madeleine placed hers over it as she had when the first of the hate mail had arrived before my exoneration.

CHAPTER FIVE

Athens's toxic pall had been cleared by a persistent wind from the Aegean Sea. From the plane the city spread broadly to the sea and to the mountains behind. Like most tourists, we wanted to see the Acropolis and Parthenon, and at different times, we each thought we had seen it first. There was no mistaking the real thing when it came into view. It seemed that everything modern beneath could never equal it.

We were stiff from the flight and flustered from being constantly jostled as we waited for our luggage. Finally, we boarded a crowded bus for the port of Piraeus. On the wharves, assaulted by the blast of ships' whistles and the constant smell of diesel, we bought our tickets to Kos at a derelict box where an elderly man in a once-white singlet sat slumped on a stool. As he spoke, I was fixated on the stains beneath his armpits. The ship would be leaving in 10 minutes, we were told in awkward English, a fact that Madeleine noted as a sign that this journey was "meant to be".

We eyed the docked ferries with approval – Minoan, Blue

Star. They were big, modern and looked sleek and beautiful in the sun and I felt satisfied that we had elected to take a ferry rather than a connecting flight. This was my concession to a new way of life, to being more spontaneous and savouring the moment. Everything seemed to be falling into place.

Our ferry was the furthest away. When we got closer, we stopped and gripped each other's elbows. A small gasp escaped Madeleine's lips. The ferry was small, old and ugly and my mind spun at the thought that we were to spend 12 hours on it. Madeleine became subdued. Her adventurous nature did not include sinking into the sea in a rusty boat.

"It might be better aboard," I said, as much to boost my own morale as hers. It wasn't.

"But I'm sure the crew will be friendly," I added, as we walked up the gangplank.

They weren't.

On board, we ate a hasty meal of limp salad and sour feta cheese as soon as the kitchen opened and then slunk down to our cabin in the hope of oblivious sleep. The Aegean Sea in late April was wild and, I discovered, on the top bunk, with the ceiling edging ever closer to my nose, that it was not just claustrophobia I was suffering from, but a literal sinking feeling that we were headed into danger.

In the dark, Kos looked even more sinister than Kalymnos. We waited on deck with the other eight passengers due to disembark; two women, one with a teenage son and the other carrying string bags full of groceries, while the rest were men of varying ages.

A thick silence rested over our heads as we waited for the

gangplank to be lowered. When it was, the others walked purposefully into their lives, leaving us to the mercy of the accommodation touts.

CHAPTER SIX

KOS

Hunger woke me. When I opened my eyes, it took some time to adjust mentally to the unfamiliarity of the room before the events of the early morning fell into place.

Surviving the ferry had given Madeleine a renewed appreciation for living. Confidently, she had steered us past the touts and into the dark at the end of the dock; I'd been grateful for it – my own attempt at being intrepid was rapidly fading. But when the hotels she'd circled in the Lonely Planet guide greeted us with firmly secured doors, her confidence had waned.

In a final attempt at leadership, but too tired to speak, I indicated with my head towards a park bench on the foreshore, visible under a solitary streetlight. We removed our packs with a thud and sat down heavily.

Across the still water, the harbour lights of Bodrum glittered and, above it, in a sky the blue of a royal robe, a sickle moon and star shone in a stunning cliché. We sat in silence, absorbing the beauty of it.

There was a flurry of movement behind us – a car screeching into the curb, an elderly man and woman almost falling out of the front seats. She strode with surprising agility ahead of him and was turning pages in a catalogue before she had even reached us. Stultified from lack of sleep, I motioned to Madeleine to follow them.

The back of the old Renault was crammed with papers, small boxes and clothing that had been shoved aside to allow room for tourists' backsides. Madeleine and I sat low to the ground while the couple in front seemed to be perched in the air. I have no memory of the husband's face, just a sense of his anxiety under the command of his wife. The greying hair beneath his bald spot sat unevenly over his collar, made worse by the tilt of his hunched shoulders.

In the rear-view mirror, I glimpsed sad and apologetic-looking eyes. He ground through the gears and the car finally took off, though there was an odd feeling of wading through thick water. I relaxed back into the peeling leather of the seat. Exhaustion released me into their hands and a sense of recklessness.

Why stop now? I thought.

After only 10 minutes, we turned into the drive of a modern complex and drove past a swimming pool to the back of the building. The rest is a tired blur of choosing beds in a small but tidy unit, of dropping luggage and climbing, fully clothed, under the bed covers.

With my chin still tucked securely beneath the stiff sheet, I scanned the room. In the other bed, Madeleine's back rose and fell in a calm sleep. To my left, large glass doors opened on to a small but functional balcony. Beyond the glass was a barren land, covered in stones and small, dense shrubs in a limited range of brown and olive green. Scattered here and there were new housing projects that were in various stages of completion, but nearly all were a white that screamed from the brown landscape surrounding it. I imagined that, from the air, these building might look like the droppings of a giant prehistoric bird. In its raw and uncontrived way, it was beautiful.

Smudges on the glass doors distracted my attention. When I focussed on them, their random placement seemed to order themselves into an opaque and transparent mosaic that drew forward the memory of another dream I'd had in the early morning.

Before Bonnie's death I remember having only dreamless sleep. Since that day, I had come to feel that I was living part of my life caught somewhere between the vivid world of dreams and waking. In this recent one, I struggled to free myself from within a room with walls of the same mosaic pattern. Their texture though, was membranous, and they bent to the pressure of my hand. Afraid that I would suffocate, I picked and prised at one raised corner of the pattern and peeled away a diamond-shaped flap that I realised, with horror, was skin.

"Can you believe that sleep?" Madeleine's voice broke my thoughts.

I rolled to face her, and we smiled with peaceful satisfaction.

"I'd like to go back into Kos Town and have a look at it in the clear light of day. What do you think?" I asked.

"Sounds good to me." Madeleine stretched and leapt from the bed with a return of her typical energy. "What did that hoverfly of a woman say about the hot water?"

"Something about the switch in there." I nodded towards the wardrobe facing us.

With 30 minutes and two cold showers behind us, we set off for Kos Town.

Outside our unit, we took in the exterior of the complex that had flashed by us in the dark. Like others, it was finished in a brilliant whitewash – hard on the eyes in those places where the midmorning sun reflected. Though we couldn't see any other tenants, there were signs of their lives – colourful beach towels over balcony rails, shampoo bottles just visible through opaque bathroom windows. At the front, the large swimming pool would have looked inviting if it wasn't for the tiny white-caps that were forming in the strong breeze that was blowing up the hill toward us.

The main road was about 100 metres down the drive, and, on its other side, the sea was just visible through the roadside trees. It wasn't the vivid blue I had expected but looked churned and dirty in the wind.

"Are they really gum trees?" I pointed ahead.

"Yes! But here?" Madeleine was disappointed.

When we reached the road, there was nothing that resembled a bus stop, but 200 metres to our left, in an open-air restaurant, a tall figure was moving between tables, setting up for lunchtime trade. As we approached, I leafed through my pocket dictionary, but before I could say a word the figure, a young man, called his hello.

We returned it.

"Hellooo Ossie!" he boomed again, "Gedayyy Maite!"

Bewildered, we introduced ourselves and he told us loudly, in fractured English, that his name was Alexander, that there was indeed a bus stop and that the bus was due any minute. We noted the menu for a later time, thanked him and headed back up the road.

"No whurrries, Ossie!" he called after us, "Come back for meal! Ask for Alexander... Alexander the Great."

"No worries!" we called back, certain that we would eat there in the future.

CHAPTER SEVEN

O n cue, the bus arrived full of young, tanned tourists of various nationalities. We jostled our way past long, sandalled legs and backpacks and took a seat at the rear.

"It seems we're staying in the Psalidi area," Madeleine looked up from the map in the guide, "Further on from us there are hot springs..." She stretched her legs in front of her and gave a soft, wistful groan.

"We'll look into getting a car today," I said, thinking that my own muscles would be grateful for the springs. I'd noticed a hire place not far from Alexander's restaurant.

"We'll check out Kos Town first though and drive back... home." How strange the word sounded to me then. Our little unit would be "home" for the time being and the thought sat well. I looked at Madeleine who, it seemed, had also noted the significance. She gently elbowed me and smiled.

"We're here," I said, returning her smile. "We made it."

Through the grimy windows of the bus, we took in the flat salt marshes as they rolled to the sea to our right and the brown and rocky hills to our left. Along the way, hotels clustered to take advantage of the sea. On a stony beach close to the road, empty deck chairs waited for hotel patrons. Further on, the roadside thickened with restaurants situated among plane trees, palms and purple bougainvillea. To the right, as we approached the fort, I saw the park bench where we had been "abducted" in the early hours of the morning. Across the water to Turkey, Bodrum was a white smear that spread from its harbour to the bare brown shoulders of its hills.

I sought the sickle moon, wanting it to be our talisman for the journey. It was still faintly visible, its two points facing west. A waxing moon, I thought, an age-old sign of fertility and propitious times. But that was in the southern hemisphere, I remembered. In the north, this was a waning moon.

The road veered between the fort on our right and large Venetian-styled buildings on our left. Already, at 11 o'clock, the pavements and the bridge above us that joined the town to the fort were filling with tourists and locals. The driver pulled the bus into a bend in front of the large open-air square that was packed with rattan tables and chairs. We had passed it all in the dark, but it had been hidden from us by our fear and exhaustion.

As we stepped on to the footpath, we were enveloped by air thick with the smell of diesel, fish, char-grilled octopus and roasted coffee beans. There were sounds of laughter, good-humoured shouting, the high-pitched whine of motor-scooters, fishermen yelling to each other and the thud of moored boats nudging. Sunlight refracted through olive oil and diesel vapour reflected off concrete pavements, whitewashed walls and harbour water. The town glowed in that light.

Holding each other's arms and tucking in our rears as a

scooter whipped behind us, we crossed the road to the harbour. Boats of all shapes and sizes jostled at its edge. The large, modern ones looked arrogantly down their long prows at the working boats below. In various stages of disrepair, these little locals rocked enthusiastically, nudging each other like the local boys when long-legged girls ambled by the quay.

For the next half hour, we skirted the harbour taking in the town, exchanged some dollars for Euros and mentally noted other practical needs – laundromats, pharmacies, general stores and smaller cafés with cheaper prices. But on our first day we resolved to eat and spend large. We crossed back to the main square and were steered by a restaurant hawker to an outdoor table.

In only half an hour I had devoured a vegetable moussaka as though it was my last meal and relaxed into the high-backed rattan armchair. Madeleine was still savouring grilled sardines in tomato and caper sauce. She was relaxed and I realised how much the adventurer in her needed to be appeased. Already my sister was fusing with the locals.

People frequently commented on our similarity, but I could only see our physical differences. Madeleine's olive skin compared to my fairer version was already deepening as we sat in the spring sun. Her large, dark-brown eyes betrayed vulnerability, despite her bursts of extroverted enthusiasm. I wondered if my own unremarkable blue-grey eyes had glazed to form another barrier to the world. We were of similar height, but Madeleine was more solid from years of physical work. At 35, she still worked as hard as the young apprentices she trained in horticulture and landscaping.

I closed my eyes enjoying the sun's warmth on my face and

arms and let the sounds of the restaurant filter through – the clink of glasses meeting in salute or being swept together by a busy waiter; conversations blending into an indistinguishable murmur, punctuated now and then by a bellowing laugh.

I opened my eyes and took in the other patrons. At one table, four men of stocky build and weighty gold jewellery were in animated conversation, gesticulating to each other. If they hadn't been laughing, I would have thought they were arguing. At another table, a raven-haired man in his thirties was entertaining two attractive Nordic-looking girls. The dark curls of his hair framed a sharp, narrow face. When serious, or listening intently, he tilted his head back and looked down his impressively long, aquiline nose. From my side view, this made him look arrogant and hard, but when he smiled or laughed, his face transformed into something to behold – like a euphoric drug, an aphrodisiac. Certainly, the body language of the girls with him suggested that they thought so, and I too found it hard to take my eyes off him.

He was a charmer and everything about him exuded confidence and sensuality. His movements were languid and graceful – the crossing of his long legs, the stretching and folding of his arms and elegant hands behind his head.

"Dee... Dana! Ooohh, my God, he's gorgeous!" Madeleine's eyes had followed mine.

At this point in our lives, my sister and I were both single. She searched for the soulmate who eluded her, but I'd never believed in the concept until I met Julian. I quickly diverted the thought.

"Greek, do you think?"

Madeleine considered him "Possibly. He could be Spanish or Italian... let's ask him."

In the middle of my grimace, he rose and cupped and kissed the face of each of the girls in turn. He left them twittering at the table and headed in our direction with a slight limp. Holding my breath, I gave my sister a light kick – a warning not to open her mouth.

"Ciao, signorine."

As he passed, he granted us a dazzling smile.

"Ciao," we said in unison, and far too loudly.

We paid for our meal and wandered deeper into the square and its tributary lanes filled with souvenir shops that sold small, white statues and busts of Hippocrates, scrolls of the Oath and other selected sayings. The merchandising was overwhelming, and I felt foolish at my romantic ideas about visiting his homeland.

Madeleine placed her hand on my back. "Let's find his tree." She perused the guidebook in her other hand looking for the route to the famous icon.

"This way." She nodded to our left.

We negotiated only a few lanes uphill until we came to Platanou Square, a small but beautiful park-like setting with plane trees and palms, cobbled paths, remnants of ancient buildings and beautiful restaurants with terraces draped in bougainvillea. Here, the air was still and though the terraces were filled with diners, they seemed hushed and muted in this space.

It wasn't difficult to find the famous plane tree, though it was fenced off and supported by scaffolding. Undoubtedly it was old – though not as old as the Koans would have tourists believe. The thought was sobering, and I wondered if there was anything authentic left on this island.

I sat on the edge of the low wall that surrounded it and contemplated the peace of the square, taking in the ancient

Turkish sarcophagus a few metres away, and the bridge to the main entrance to the fort—the Castle of the Knights.

"I'm going for a stroll." Madeleine headed toward the bridge, leaving me to daydream.

Whether Hippocrates had taught under this plane tree or not, the square had seen much of the life of ancient Kos Town. Most certainly he would have walked here, perhaps deep in a thought or conversation that would ultimately change the practice of Western medicine. I turned to face the tree, picturing him walking with his students. I waited for a feeling – that I would find an answer to a need I could not yet identify. Was I right to come here? There was a rustle in the leaves as I mentally posed my question, but nothing more.

On the bridge, I joined Madeleine, who was studying the sign on the double gates into the castle.

"Too late today – we're locked out," she said.

"Yes," I said, "I could believe that."

An hour later, and with basic supplies, we walked back along the avenue to a car-hire outlet I had seen from the bus. We left in a Fiat – freedom in canary yellow.

When we arrived at our complex in the late afternoon, we wondered if the signs of life we had seen in the morning were just props arranged by our hoverfly and husband. Once inside, I could see, on the neighbouring balcony rail, two pairs of feminine feet that flexed expressively with the animated conversation of their owners.

We ate a light tea of Greek salad and local wine on our own balcony and soaked in the atmosphere that was free of wind and sound. In the dusk, the hills turned from brown to grey and, as night set in, the lights in the condominiums were matched with stars. Lulled by the peace and our full stomachs, we reviewed our journey so far and decided that, perhaps, it was not a mistake to come after all.

As the evening turned cooler, I left Madeleine to contemplate the view and went inside. I took out the collected material on Hippocrates and, for the next hour, searched through the books on the bed looking for something that would resonate to my core or shake the foundation from under me.

Under that stark, naked bulb of my Kos bedroom, I gained a better appreciation than I had ever had of his influence on Western medicine, that he had taken its practice out of the hands of the priests who loaded their patients with guilt and brought rational understanding to the cause and treatment of many diseases. I understood more deeply that his influence had extended through the generations of medical training, and had been fundamental to my own, but there was a new recognition in me, that something was missing. I felt dry.

Madeleine tiptoed in and, without speaking, sank into bed. After another fruitless hour, accompanied by my sister's soft snoring, I thought that perhaps Hippocrates could not be truly known through the written word, but would need to be experienced in his homeland.

CHAPTER EIGHT

The wind that had whipped up the sea the day before had eased, and the Aegean was its trademark blue. As we began our ascent, the view was stunning and the cape, where the island's mountain chain came to a rugged end, had the look of a racked and life-beaten soul. On a small plateau, before the descent to the hot springs of Thermes, wild goats grazed while their kids played in the stones and tufts of the coastal grasses.

I pulled into a car park to join two other hire cars. From the top of the worn and precarious staircase we could see four women lying in the shallows where hot water seeped through small vents near the shore. We descended, gripping at the rusted and brittle rail. The sheer cliff face opposite us loomed over the stony beach. Here, the seep of hot water at the cliff's base reminded me of the awesome force that lay beneath, like the tic of a madman.

If my sister was threatened by this brutal beauty, she didn't appear so. No sooner had we chosen our place among the pebbles than she was stripping to her bathers and tottering barefoot to the vaporising shallows. She had already taken up position with the other women when I reached the water that immediately fizzed around my feet.

The prone, silent women unnerved me, and when they opened their eyes to take me in, I self-consciously lowered myself into the water's warmth and lay on my back next to Madeleine.

It was a surreal moment, lying in silence in a type of sisterhood with the women, and I wondered if we were re-enacting a similar scene two-and-a-half thousand years earlier. As I lay in the sulphurous balm, I took in those boulders that lay at the cliff's feet and looked for their origins on the face, tracking my eyes up and up to the towering summit and to the impossibly blue sky. I closed my eyes and felt the warmth seeping into my limbs, the sulphur into my nose and I imagined myself slowly disassembling in this stew, returning my molecules to the whole.

I felt weightless, borderless. Through my hooded lids, I took in again the summit of the cliff and saw a movement among the straggling vegetation. A small rock dislodged and trickled to a shelf below. When I looked up again, a mountain goat stood looking out to sea.

Madeleine continued to meditate in her bath, but two of the other women began to murmur softly to each other in German. I closed my eyes again and soaked up the heat, the peace and the sound of them, and thought of my childhood holidays spent on the beaches of one of Melbourne's own peninsulas.

I thought of the hours spent swimming in the bay during the seemingly endless summer days of my youth and how, exhausted from swimming, I would throw myself on to the sand and listen to the sounds of the beach – the gulls fighting each other over the scraps from someone's fishing bucket; of other children playing in the water's safe aqua zone, and the drumming of the hulls of hire boats anchored just offshore. I remembered that freedom, the complete happiness of it. And I felt it here too, in the hot springs of a foreign island.

For the rest of that day, our muscles revived and feeling a luxurious calm, we toured the length of the island, marvelling at its history, in awe of the olive trees that resembled the animated trees of fantasy. Cultivated in groves hundreds of years before and now growing wild, they would have been witness to generations of change. When we returned at sunset, we decided to try out our local restaurant. Alexander greeted us with the same effusive enthusiasm as he had the previous day.

"Geddayyyy Ossies!"

Madeleine was intrigued. "Alexander, how do you know we're Australian?"

He looked at her in mock bewilderment.

"How you talk! Must be how you look!" he said, waving his arms up and down. He guided us to an outdoor table.

"Do we really sound like that?" Madeleine persisted.

"No whurrreees," Alexander laughed. "When I was in Melborrrne," he confided, "everybody," he added, moving his arms like windmills to make his point, "speak same."

"You've been to Melbourne?" I said, the world feeling smaller to me all the time.

"Of course! My aunteee, uncle, my cousins all live there. I stay for six month... for geology."

"Geology?"

"Alexander is not just a fabulous waiter," he boasted. "I also nearly a geologist."

I stored this information away for the moment thinking of the tiny stone stored in my room.

"Why do you come all the way to Kos?"

Between us Madeleine and I told him, in our broken version of English that we had come to learn about Hippocrates.

"Ahhhh, great man," Alexander said dreamily," but, for me, not so great as Asklepios."

I knew that Asklepios had been worshipped by Hippocrates, who honoured the god in the first line of his Oath, and that he was included in the recounting of Hippocrates' dream that I had read on the plane. I thought that I knew him, too, from another source, but couldn't think of it then.

"He was greatest healer," Alexander continued, "long, long time. Even before great battle of Troy." A family arrived and he apologised as he left to attend to them.

"Interesting," Madeleine said, spreading hummus on thick slices of bread.

"Yes." Asklepios, I resolved, would have my attention.

Back in the room, while Madeleine introduced herself to the "feet" next door, I resumed my research, from a different angle. The books in my possession made only fleeting reference to Asklepios and there seemed to be some confusion whether he had been a man or a god. His origins, though, were in Thessaly and there was a temple dedicated to him there, in Epidaurus and in Kos at the site known as the Asklepion. Although Asklepios had been worshipped on Kos, and that Hippocrates himself was an Asklepiad – a supposed descendant – the younger physician was the main hero of this island. The next day, I decided, I would go to the Asklepion.

CHAPTER NINE

"I need some retail therapy," my sister announced the next morning. "From what I've read, Bodrum's the place for it, and only 30 minutes away by ferry."

The morning sky held the promise of a sunny day and I told her of my plans to visit the Asklepion. "Have a rest," she said, "and don't overdo it."

After dropping Madeleine off at the quay, I wound my way through the streets of Kos Town, through the Turkish Platani area with its traditional tavernas, complete with blue-and-white check tablecloths and vine-strewn pergolas, to the Asklepion, four kilometres out of town. As I pulled into the car park, my heart sank at the sight of two large tourist buses already there. I bought a ticket and map and followed the signed path that opened suddenly on to a clearing in the hillside.

Standing at its base, I took in the three terraced levels of the Asklepion that unrolled ahead of me to the top of the hill. From where I stood, I could see that each level was littered with ruins of temples. Some pillars were still standing, but most were lying where they had fallen centuries before. The sightseers from the buses were milling over the levels in a fine stream up the central staircases, or in small groups huddled around a tour guide. And yet, there was a pervading sense of quiet.

On the first terrace, the Romans had left their trademark – the remnants of a large bathing house. In recesses of a retaining wall, headless statues stood with authority. In one small grotto, a maidenhair fern had found its niche beneath the glare of a lion's head where a mineral rich spring spewed from its mouth. I climbed the 20 steps to the second terrace. To my left stood colonnades – the remnants of the temple to Apollo – to my right, the altar to Asklepios. It consisted merely of a large slab of marble supported by thick rectangular stones. I stood before the altar and ran my hand over it, wondering what had been offered there more than 2,500 years earlier. I closed my eyes for a moment and was startled by the pungent and unpleasant smell of fish.

For two hours, I wandered the terraces, consulting my paper guide and tagging tour groups to catch some more detailed accounts in my rudimentary understanding of German and French. Every now and then thick, dark clouds would cause a light and shade strobing that accentuated the dramatic feel of the place.

On the large retaining wall of the third terrace, I sat like a child with my legs dangling over the edge as I took in the spectacular view of Kos Town, the sea and the coast of Asia Minor. Out there, the world, including my sister no doubt, moved at a frenetic pace, but this place was a peaceful core. Everyone seemed to sense it, talking in muted tones, or just sitting alone or with others in silence. In the cypress grove that buffered the two worlds, I read, birth and death had been forbidden.

Beneath my dangling feet were the remnants of the abaton – the rooms where the sick would come to sleep. It was here, in their dreams, that Asklepios would appear and advise them of a cure. I marvelled at such simple faith, but thought, too, of the tragic repercussions when that faith was misplaced. I had left elements of my life behind in Melbourne, but Bonnie travelled with me. I wondered where and how I was to heal.

I was drawn now to the rooms beneath me and descended the stairs to sit alone among the ruins almost hidden in the grass. The dark clouds were colluding and forming a thick, menacing ceiling. Where I sat on the remnants of a stone wall, I ran my finger into its nicks and recesses, imagining an ancient hand fashioning it in honour of the god. This site was built after the death of Hippocrates, but it was Asklepios and Apollo who were worshipped here.

At my feet, tiny wildflowers grew – purple with yellow centres. The longer I looked at them the larger they appeared until I felt myself drawn to them. A bee rested delicately on stamens, and I became mesmerised by the humming of its wings. I wasn't aware of falling asleep, only the weight of my head, a heaviness of my limbs and a sense of stupor covering my scattering thoughts in fur.

I remember blurred images – imperfect apples, olives and wheat placed with love on a marble table in front of me; fish that now seemed pleasant and whole and organic, and shells fashioned into necklaces. I saw the sick in their beds waiting with trust for their cure. I felt their fear, their maladies. I reached forward to one and touched her barren womb and tracked my way to her troubled heart. In her sleep, she wept. For another I pricked his skin and tongue with nettle to clean the black from his blood. And then I saw myself lie down, to dream of a cure for my troubled soul. The heavens roared and a spear of light jagged its way across the sky to find me.

I must have yelled. When I opened my eyes, a couple was watching me warily. I feigned indifference and stood and stretched. Though the sky was becoming dark there was only a very distant rumble of thunder, but I wasted no time in returning to the safety of the little canary.

"You look awful."

"Thanks for that," I said, knowing well that Madeleine was right. "How was your day?"

There was a heightened sparkle in my sister's eyes that sounded a warning bell in me.

"So, who is he?" I said, not taking her by surprise at all.

"You won't believe this," she said, unfazed and her face breaking into a large and beautiful smile. She laughed at my bemused eyebrow. "No, really you won't."

"Try me," I said, now intrigued.

"Remember that Adonis chatting up the Nordic beauties at the restaurant in Kos?"

"Not him!" I almost yelled. Madeleine was wrong. I did believe her and that's what I was worried about.

"Oh yes indeed," her smile was smug, "Carlo Augustus Giorni."

"He told you his middle name!" I imagined him rolling it into my sister's all-too-receptive ear.

"He's a dream." Madeleine's sparkle was turning into a mist.

There have been many times when I felt like shaking my sister, and this was one of them. Already, I was imagining the heartbroken scenario when our Latin lover moved on or, more typically, when Madeleine became bored.

"He's a racing-car driver," she said, matter-of-factly, cutting across my thoughts.

"Oh, for God's sake!"

"Famous in Europe." She was goading me now.

We laughed.

"And he's coming here for dinner tomorrow night!"

Together we turned and assessed the apartment as if seeing it for the first time.

———

Madeleine related her day. She had met the famous Carlo in the lounge of the ferry. As she quietly sipped her coffee, gazing innocently out the window, the racing car driver of exquisite reflexes and timing stumbled towards her on his way past as the ferry rode a rogue wave. The rest, I could imagine. Despite a foot injury, sustained during a recent Grand Prix – I rolled my eyes – Carlo Augustus Giorni accompanied my sister on her day's shopping. Scarves, jewellery and two summer shirts in a blast of colour were spread on the bed.

"I bought you this," she said, holding out her arm, her fist closed to hide its contents. "Actually, Carlo saw it first, but the man in the shop insisted that I buy it and – this is the weird thing – give it to my sister. A lucky guess, I'd say."

In my palm, she placed a beautiful yet tiny container – a vial, of exquisite workmanship. It was made of alabaster with a delicate filigree-of-gold casing and was sealed tightly by a lid that tapered to a point.

"Dana, are you OK?"

My sister's voice drew me from a kaleidoscope of images that I could not make sense of.

"It's the myrrh," I said, "beautiful, but a bit heady for me at first."

Madeleine looked confused. She took the vial from me and sniffed around the seal. When she looked at me her eyes were full of concern.

"Dee, it's empty."

CHAPTER TEN

In my dream, the images of the day visited me in their distortions. Again, the membranous walls surrounded me, though the light that came through was of a different, softer hue and the wall met the floor in a concave arch. Among the panes, I recognised one whose corner I had previously begun to peel, though it seemed now to be set higher in the wall and I had to stand on my toes to reach it. It felt rigid, almost brittle in my hand and, when I pressed at the lower panes, they, too, were hard and unyielding.

Confused, I stood in the centre of the room, bathed in dreamy sunset colours, wondering where I had seen a similar effect before, and was reminded of a large alabaster window in the Vatican City. Turning full circle in my prison, I realised, with rising fear, that I was inside the vial. A shadow skirted the outside and came close enough for me to make out the impression of legs as they leaned against the wall.

Desperate to be free, I rushed forward but stopped, rigid with fear when a long-fingered hand reached through the peeled corner of the pane. It flexed in an urgent invitation for me to clasp it. I scaled the concave interior toward it, my eyes fixed on that hand and the blue and gold ring on the long, third finger. As I stretched forward a voice behind me yelled a warning. Stunned, I slid to the floor and spun around.

Standing in the middle of the room, his face locked in an urgent call, was Julian. In the glow of the alabaster panes, he was like an apparition, and I strained my eyes to determine a body of substance. His face, full of consternation, called me silently to him, though his eyes flicked from my own to the wall behind me. Remembering the hand, I turned to see it slip in surrender from the opening, and the silhouetted form of its owner evaporate into the light. When I turned back to Julian, he too had gone.

My longing to see Julian gnawed at me in tiny bites. When he'd left for London only weeks before Bonnie's death, I'd tried to block him from my thoughts by working at a frenetic pace. I didn't want a long-distance relationship, I'd told him; I wouldn't jeopardise what I'd worked for by going with him, I'd said. In truth, I'd hoped he would stay, to give up his own opportunity as head of a neuroscience unit in a progressive London hospital.

Since Bonnie, he'd called from London twice a week to make sure I was all right and offered to come back for a few weeks to support me. I'd refused. His last call had left me flattened when I realised how much I missed his warmth and practical advice; how the measured timbre of his voice seemed to resonate within me. He spoke animatedly of his life in London, and I doubted that there was room for me anymore.

I decided that I would write to tell him that I was in Kos. He would be hurt that I didn't call him and that I had not answered any of his messages; I tried to avoid the emotional drain of speaking with him. When I'd heard people talk of the need for closure in relationships, I was irked by the pseudo-psychological language, but Julian and I needed to move on.

I was grateful for the distraction when Madeleine and I shopped for the evening meal in an indoor marketplace alive with the sounds of bargain trading and with colourful produce. A priority purchase was the Kos lettuce with tomatoes, feta cheese, olives, bread and freshly made dips, fishcakes, cold meat and saganaki cheese.

"I hope he's not a vegan," Madeleine said.

I doubted it, I said, and kept to myself the thought that Carlo had the look of a carnivore.

My sister seemed to be quite calm about the prospect of the evening, while I felt put out. I suspected it was because I was disapproving, a character trait of which I was becoming increasingly aware. Where I had thought that my life, compared to Madeleine's, was ordered and sensible, now, in her constant presence, and on this island so far away from home, I saw myself as being wound too tightly. I could blame the preceding months, but I suspected that the reel had been winding for some time.

Had Julian seen it? On the day he left for London, he said: "Be open, Dana, to the possibility of us."

The words had stung, and I had replayed them often. I thought I had been open to possibility. I'd proven myself in a largely male-dominated profession. I'd thought that I was open to the future of our relationship until he took up a position overseas. We'd ended it, but only because I didn't want him to feel obligated to me and there was no chance of us living together for some years yet. I rolled the thoughts around, still feeling a rise of indignation, but time was tempering it now.

———

As the time for our guest's arrival came closer, the nonchalant attitude my sister had veiled herself in during the day was shredding. Twice she nearly sliced her finger instead of the tomatoes, and I had to rescue the lettuce from being torn to tragic shreds. I offered to fry the saganaki cheese when the time came, conscious that anything involving heat, oil and precision frying would be beyond her.

Perversely, the more hyped Madeleine became, the more I relaxed. A strange harmonic seemed to be at work. By the time the knock at the door came, she was tightly strung. Where I would have looked stricken and strained, my eyes just "burnt holes in a blanket", as my mother would say, the adrenalin rush heightened my sister's beauty. Face flushed and eyes alight, Madeleine glowed, and I became acutely aware that my role in this evening's tryst was the spinsterly chaperone.

While the effect of the knock was to root Madeleine's feet to the floor, I offered to open the door, exaggerating the straightness of my back in case I had suddenly developed a dowager's hump. Though I was not looking forward to meeting him, when I opened the door, my breath caught in my throat. Carlo Augustus Giorni was... beautiful, and when he flashed his perfect teeth in sexy pirate fashion, I had to scold my heart for its tiny palpitation. This was a man, I decided, who must never be trusted. The thought caused me to turn quickly to my sister in warning, but she was now moving in an almost ethereal manner to the door. Madeleine was beguiled, enchanted and heading straight to disaster. I stepped aside.

"Ciao, signorine... Ciao, Madeleina." Cheek kisses were

47

traded between them; presents appeared from behind Carlo's back. As he presented yellow roses to my sister, my eyes were drawn to his hand – long, slender fingers and, on the third, the blue and gold ring of my dream.

"Dana."

Madeleine's voice broke my reverie as she introduced us.

"Ciao, Dana... bella... like your sister." I saw his lips moving, but I was submerged in my thoughts, taking in his face, the hands, the ring.

"Dana!" This time a bit sharper from Madeleine, who gave me a quizzical and not-too-loving look.

I extended my hand, remembering that I had done so in my dream. This time they met, no Julian to sound a warning behind me. I wished that I could now turn and see his face.

Ushering our guest through the kitchen – the hoverfly had not seen a need for chairs – the three of us sat, awkwardly, physically and mentally, on the twin single beds. I wondered if this was the fastest invitation our "racy" car driver had ever had to the bedroom. Heightening my third-party paranoia, Madeleine and Carlo sat on her bed opposite me, our feet meeting in a sorry little shuffle in the small floor space between us. I jumped up and went to the balcony, returning noisily and inelegantly with the small outdoor table that I placed with too much gusto in that awkward space between us.

In spite of this, perhaps in spite of me, the evening meal was relaxed and pleasant. Carlo ate passionately and appreciatively. He proved to be an interested and charming guest. Madeleine ate little, her appetite sated by some inner fuel. What surprised me was the apparently genuine affection between them. Was this the Italian's guise? I held my suspicions. Carlo Augustus Giorni was indeed a racing car driver and had won several Grand Prix. Although it would have been easy to fool the two of us, there was nothing flashy in the recounting of his life on the track and he spoke with the uncontrived modesty of the successful. At times, he seemed almost reluctant to discuss his profession and I wondered if it was because of a deeper dissatisfaction.

Over coffee and baklava, we talked of our different reasons for coming to Kos. For Carlo, it was simply to rest his injured foot and, I wondered, a life disillusionment that became more apparent as the evening progressed. In my sister's company, he seemed to relax, and some hyperactive edges softened. Madeleine, too, seemed to be at ease at last.

Over the course of the evening, I came to envy what I thought was happening between them – genuine friendship and affection that held the potential for love. I envied it because I had known it.

"Your ring," I said casually, "it's very beautiful, and unusual."

Carlo splayed his fingers and regarded it.

"Is old... given me from my grandfather."

"It looks Greek or Byzantine."

"The history is lost, but, Dana, you correct," he said, looking impressed "Grandfather was Greek, from Thessaly."

Carlo's gaze shifted from his ring to our humble room.

"Ah... Madeleina... the vial."

My hand moved protectively toward the tiny vial on my bedside table.

"It's lovely," I said, placing it on the table between us. "Madeleine told me you found it on the market stall."

"Sì," he said, in that nonchalant way of the Italians.

Madeleine picked it up. "Wasn't it strange, Carlo, the way that man insisted I have it, and that I give it to my sister?"

"Sì, Madeleina." Only now did Carlo look away from the vial and, I noted regarded my sister with genuine affection. "Old man... still enchanted by beautiful woman."

She blushed. I looked at her with wonder, realising that I was witnessing the intimacy of her relationships. The insight was humbling because this was a side of her that I didn't really know. At that moment, I felt both distanced from and closer to her and I wondered how she would see me in the same situation.

I extracted myself from their heady company and carried the dishes to the kitchen to ponder the coincidences of the day. With the perspective of two glasses of wine, I reasoned that Carlo's ring must have been visible to me on that first sighting in the restaurant; that the alabaster room of my dream was prompted by the vial, and that my imprisonment, the hand and the presence of Julian, were fashioned from some deep psychological need I couldn't yet label.

Interrupting the hesitant intimacies in the next room, I collected my Glad Bag sachet that contained the stone, rugged up for the crisp Kos night and headed to our resident geologist in the local taverna.

CHAPTER ELEVEN

A few customers were sitting over their coffee and digestifs. Alexander, at the back of the restaurant, looked up and waved when he saw me. Gracefully, he manoeuvred his lanky frame between the tables. A real pro, I thought.

"Osseee!" From his beaming face, the term was endearing. "You eat late tonight?"

"Just a coffee, Alexander, if that's OK, and... a favour."

He looked perplexed.

I laughed. "I have a question".

"Ne... I get coffee and you ask me favorrr."

I brought out my sachet and laid the tiny stone on a paper serviette. When Alexander returned with my coffee, he eyed it with curiosity. I offered him a seat opposite me. Madeleine and I had previously told him the outline of our odyssey to Kos, and I filled in some of the details, beginning with the stone, though I only hazily sketched the circumstance under which it had arrived.

"Can you tell me what type of material it is?" I said, as he rolled the stone between his fingers.

His expression was serious, concentrated and I was allowed an insight into a very different Alexander to the talkative and breezy waiter I had come to know.

"Marble," he said, confirming my own guess. He leaned forward with it still in his palm. "See... here..." He pointed to the pink markings. "Unusual."

"Would I be able to find out where it's from?" I leaned closer. From the corner of my eye, I could see a patron regarding us with curiosity.

He leaned back, rolling the stone almost lovingly. "Maybe can do... it will take time, Ossee... I'm going to Athens tomorrow. Mind if I take?"

I felt a rush of protectiveness of my small talisman.

"Ne," I said, feeling relieved that I might finally find out something. "I'd appreciate it."

For another hour over coffee, and between Alexander clearing tables and farewelling the other patrons, I got to know more about our local and favourite waiter – his dreams of teaching at the University of Athens, of marrying his childhood sweetheart who was studying there, too.

"Alexander, why are you here in Kos?"

He laughed, "To get away from everything for a while."

I nodded. I understood.

At home, Madeleine was on her own, washing dishes and looking like the cat that had swallowed the bird.

"He had to go," she said, as I picked up a tea towel.

"Where's he staying?"

"I'm not sure," she said, her hands pausing in the sink. "I haven't asked. Somewhere in town, anyway."

Another difference between us, I thought.

"When are you seeing him again?"

"He wanted to see me tomorrow, but..." she said, then paused and turned to me, "I said I wanted to spend the day with my sister."

"Thanks, Mads."

———

The next day, we browsed shops in town and had a lazy lunch, walking and talking. I posted my basic, informative letter to Julian. As we climbed the steps to our flat, we could see something wedged in our door. Excitedly, Madeleine retrieved it, but her face dropped in disappointment as she handed it to me. Instantly I recognised the handwriting where she hadn't, but the expression on my face made her look again.

"Oh God... another one? But how?"

I unlocked the door and, once inside, we sat side by side on the bed as I opened the envelope. With unsteady fingers, I unfolded the letter which, I noted, was of the same paper – parchment – though the ink was of a deeper blue than before. This time, the words were unquestionably in Latin.

I translated aloud: "What you seek from me, you might have looked for nearer home." The words sounded familiar. At university, I had studied a unit of Latin for interest, alongside my medical degree. Largely, classes consisted of reading the works of Virgil and Ovid, and it was the latter that I now recalled. I repeated the words, picturing them toward the end of Ovid's Metamorphoses, and I had a feeling that they may have been about Asklepios.

"Of course," I said aloud, startling Madeleine. "I did know something of Asklepios! I have to get a copy of that book."

By now Madeleine was truly bewildered. "What book?"
I explained.

"This is getting a bit strange now, Dee," she said, trying to disguise her excitement with a fearful face.

While we waited for Alexander to return, Madeleine and I resumed our tour of the island, and of bookshops looking for Ovid. In a "junk" box in an unlikely general store in the main town, I found a battered copy. Despite its decrepit state, leafing through the pages revealed that its soul was still intact. I tucked it deep into my bag for later reading.

There had been no word from Carlo. Though Madeleine seemed to be happy enough in conversation, she drifted into daydream more often than usual. As we lingered over lunch in town, I saw him in an adjacent restaurant. Despite his sunglasses, it was apparent that he was tired, his face pale and drawn. Madeleine hadn't seen him, and I hoped that we, or he, might slip away unnoticed.

It was too late. I saw the small jerk of her body when she saw him and her brow furrowed in a mixture of annoyance and perplexity, but she remained fixed in her chair, not at all like her normally direct and open way.

"Ciao, Madeleina." Carlo's voice was soft and tired as he approached us.

My sister's smile was tight, and I found myself, again as a reluctant third party, feeling almost sorry for the Italian play-boy. I rose, making an excuse that I had to find an ATM, but neither of them seemed to notice. When I turned back to look, Carlo was easing himself tentatively and apologetically into my chair.

I wandered along the quay, stopping now and then to take in the latest arrival of cruisers and their bewildering state-of-the-art designs. Longer, stronger, leaner and bedecked with satellite dishes and plunge pools. Behind me, I heard running feet and stepped aside to allow the jogger to pass. At the tap on my shoulder, I turned to find Alexander, puffing and red-faced.

"Ossee!"

It occurred to me to tell him my name, but I was now becoming very fond of my new one. Madeleine and I had already decided that he bore a remarkable resemblance to Prince Andrew of England and now, in his impeccable casual shirt, pants and boat shoes, he looked even more like a royal on vacation.

"The stone," he said excitedly as his breathing levelled, "I have result."

It was my turn to breathe deeply.

He laughed at my expression but then became serious.

"Marble not from Kos, not from Turkei." He raised his eyebrows apologetically.

"I suppose we can't find out where it's from?"

Alexander nodded, "This particular mineral composition is most common in west."

"West?"

"Ne... Apennini."

"The Apennines," I said, conscious that I was becoming Alexander's echo. My mind ran through my limited knowledge of European geography. "That would include..."

"Italia." Alexander seemed to be following my thoughts.

"Any idea where?"

He smiled. "No guesses. Sorry, Ossee. Stone is too small." He took it from his pocket and handed it to me with great respect.

My heart sank. The information was intriguing, exciting, but we had come to a standstill. Finding the origins of my tiny stone in a number of European countries was like a needle in 10,000 haystacks. Alexander looked disappointed for me. I hugged him in gratitude. With his arms fixed to his sides, he blushed, but I noticed his wry smile.

"Pleasure, for you, Ossee," he called over his shoulder as he left.

"Thank you," I called after him.

I headed back to the restaurant. Madeleine was sitting on her own sipping the last of her orange juice.

"I'm OK," she said.

On the way home, we exchanged our stories. Carlo, it seemed, had had to fly to Athens for an urgent meeting with his manager and then to his specialist.

"Why hadn't he told you he would be going?"

"He said he'd forgotten about it."

She didn't seem to doubt him; another difference between us.

I told her about my chance meeting with Alexander.

"This is such an adventure." Madeleine's take on the situation lightened my own. We drove on. "Have you heard from Julian?"

She had asked tentatively but it jolted me.

"Not since I spoke to him before we left." I told her that I had sent him a letter.

"You should never have let him get away, Dana."

This was not the first time my sister had reminded me of this, but I couldn't help but wonder if it was now prompted by her interest in Carlo. Perhaps she thought I was getting in her way. My instinct was to launch again into my reasons for breaking up with Julian, but nothing came. I tried to distract myself with the now familiar scenery outside the car but, at that moment, it seemed drab and colourless.

The inside me and the outside me seemed to have fused.

CHAPTER TWELVE

When I woke the next morning, there was the shape of someone's name still on my lips. For months, I hadn't thought of life before Bonnie's death, a life that seemed now so far from me. In my dream, I had returned to the comforts of that life, where the smallest things made me content – early morning routines before work, the greetings of colleagues, and even the exhaustion I often felt when I finally climbed into bed after a long day. Lying there now, undecided about the day, in a foreign bed so far from home, was not a luxury. I allowed myself to slip back into sleep and searched for the comfort of my lost routines.

"Dana!"

Madeleine, showered and dressed for the day, sat close, a mug of tea held towards me as an incentive to get up.

"What will we do today?" she said. Her voice was sunny but the day behind was not.

"Let's go home, Mads."

The mug in my sister's hand jerked, spilling droplets of tea on to the bed. In slow motion, she placed it on the bedside table. Her hand, still warm from the cup, stroked my forehead. My heart surged with a great longing for the comfort of my mother's arms, though, in truth, I hadn't often felt their embrace.

"Is that what you really want?" Madeleine's question might well have been my own.

I looked beyond her to the overcast sky that was the same as those that shrouded my days in Melbourne over the last few months. It seemed there was no escaping my gloom.

"I don't know."

In the quiet hum of established rituals, we wandered the arcades. Over lunch by the quay, we considered our next move. Going home wasn't going to resolve anything for me, but I was feeling stifled here as if the sea cut off the possibility of change. Alexander's news that the stone was not from Kos heralded a sense of closure for my time on this island and I was restless now to move on.

Carlo hadn't been mentioned during the day, so I was surprised when Madeleine said he had asked her to accompany him to Rome. She had declined and he had left to attend to an urgent matter there – though he didn't tell her what that was. The mention of my favourite city stirred me enough to consider it and, by the end of the afternoon, with Madeleine in full agreement, we had tickets for Rome, leaving the next day.

"There's one thing I need to do," I told her as we headed home to pack. I steered the car back toward the town and drove, for the last time, to the Asklepion. Madeleine waited in the car while I paid for my ticket and climbed the steps to the abaton.

Again, I sat on the retaining wall and closed my eyes to the sun that had emerged from a rain-filled cloud. In my mind I heard gentle singing, a lullaby, and I felt myself lean towards vaporous arms that disassembled before me. My torso continued forward until I was wrapped about my knees in a foetal position. I opened my eyes, suddenly conscious of myself in a public place, only to find my body was sitting upright.

Frightened now, I left the Asklepion for the last time.

Through the car window, I could see my sister's lazy stretch. There was something almost feline about her long limbs that moved in elegant flexes. Many years before, when we had taken up yoga together, we shared that same flexibility. Now my muscles were strong from gym workouts, but they were tight and solid.

"How'd you go?" she said as I eased into the driver's seat.

"OK," I lied, not wanting her to be concerned any more about my emotional, and now my mental, health. "It was a bit crowded."

"So sorrree that you go," Alexander seemed genuinely sad at our news, but he nodded to me in understanding.

Though I had been impatient to leave this morning, I felt some regret now as I looked around the little taverna that had become almost as familiar as my own dining room, and I would be sorry to leave Alexander; he had become a good friend.

"See you later, Ossies," he said, as we were leaving, his exaggerated accent softer now than at our first meeting. My impulse was to hug him, and Madeleine did. Alexander blushed and turned quickly from us as if another patron had suddenly called him.

Despite the bleakness of the day, it was a beautiful night, our last in Kos. Though the air was cool as we walked back to our unit, there had been enough warmth in the day's occasional bursts of sunlight to heat the oil in the eucalyptus trees by the side of the road. Their scent came as a reminder of how far we had travelled.

CHAPTER THIRTEEN

ROME

O n the journey to Rome, I was full of apprehension and felt as though I was chasing myself across the world. There was a subtle shift of gravity in my body as the plane began its descent.

Madeleine moved in her seat and opened one eye. "OK?" Reassured, she nestled again into the woolly comfort of her jumper that served as a pillow. Over the last six months, the dynamics of our relationship had changed and had strengthened in a way that it might never have done if we had not come on this journey together. If nothing else, it was worth it just for that.

The bus trip from Fiumicino Airport was as I remembered from my first trip years earlier. I had wondered then why people loved Rome – until the bus turned into the Piazza Venezia.

"Bella..." Madeleine's sigh reflected my own thought, but I suspected there was a subtext of a different enchantment. As far as I knew, Carlo didn't know she was coming to Rome, and I wondered if he would be pleasantly surprised.

We unpacked in our hotel and took a short walk to explore our new neighbourhood, so different from what we had just left. Where the sense of space, smell and colour seemed so important in Kos, here the city might just as well have been grey. Rome was stupendous in its clutter of human endeavours. I was glad to be in a city; it seemed easier to lose myself.

We spoke little as we walked, in wonder again at piazzas crammed with fountains, statues, locals and tourists. It was just as I had remembered – crowded, noisy and beautiful and I had loved it.

When we reached the Forum, I marvelled that a city that moved at such a frenetic pace would allow the space to unearth the past. Spring was spilling across the ruins. Wildflowers grew around fallen marble columns and among the graves of ancient Caesars.

Madeleine and I leaned against the remains of a spring and drank filtered water from plastic bottles. Ahead were the Temple of Vespasianus and The Curia and tour guides strode ahead of their flocks, extolling the virtues of Roman politics and the arch. St Peter's Basilica would be the next stop, I supposed, having been on one of these tours when I came here in the days before I met Julian.

In those days, I had been content with my single life, establishing my practice with little time to socialise. Coming to Europe on my own had been a great adventure. Julian had taken me by surprise in the way that wonderful things can do when you least need or want them. I hadn't been ready for a relationship and, looking back, I realised that I had resisted it for too much of the time. He was patient. He knew the need to concentrate on establishing a profession, but he seemed better able to make room for me than I was for him.

A couple wandered past, arm in arm. The man resembled Julian, I thought with a pang, but I had been seeing versions of him in many places. He wouldn't know that we had left Kos, if he knew yet that we had been there at all.

A sparrow rested on a fallen column, shifting its body and eyeing us for food. It reminded me of the sparrows outside Deb's café; Julian could pick out the differences between them. As they pecked at abandoned toast on tables, he would point out their idiosyncrasies. I had loved that about him, his eye for small details and his breadth of interest and enthusiasm for life. They were things that I learned about him over time. He was quiet and carried an air of serenity, almost austerity, that some found intimidating, as I had when we first met at a medical conference.

Over sandwiches and muffins during the morning tea break, we found ourselves together. We exchanged a few awkward clichés and returned to our separate seats in the auditorium. At lunch, we were placed next to each other. The conference had been uninteresting, and I was more tired than I would have been after a long shift. Perhaps it gave me a flippancy I wouldn't normally have, but I found myself talking to him openly and with less inhibition than I had two hours earlier.

Looking back, it was more likely due to his patient attention. I don't remember what he had said during that lunch, but when he asked me if I would like to meet him for dinner the following week, I didn't hesitate to accept.

My mind was distracted when I answered the telephone days later. He must have heard the confusion in my voice, and I sensed his embarrassment. I'd forgotten that the evening we had arranged to meet clashed with a late-organised, but important, dinner with a benefactor of the hospital, and I couldn't miss it. Julian took my cancellation with good grace. I suggested another time, but he was busy for the next two weeks and we ended that conversation in a state of limbo.

Though work preoccupied me during that time, I found myself thinking of him in unlikely or irrelevant contexts. Although I had only seen him once, I was piecing him together from the men around me. By the end of the second week, he had the eyes of one of the hospital's radiologists, the fair hair of the electrician who installed a range hood in my kitchen, and the hands of my friend, David. I loved those hands – broad, strong, but with a slight inward curve of the little finger toward the palm that added a feminine footnote to his masculinity.

At the end of the second week, Julian rang, and I made certain that I sounded welcoming. We talked comfortably about the intervening weeks and when I suggested dinner for the next evening, he was quick to accept. I dressed carefully for that date, taking longer over little incidentals of grooming. Although he had offered to pick me up, I chose to meet him at the restaurant, so that I had the freedom to leave when I wanted to.

I didn't want to make an entrance, to allow him to study me as I came in so I arrived 15 minutes early. He was already sitting at a table by the window. His body faced me, but he was watching the passing traffic. Though he sat quite erect in the chair, his facial expression was that of relaxed confidence. His hair, not quite as sun streaked as my electrician's, was slightly longer and wavier than I had remembered and, as I approached, I noticed a small wave sat just over the stiff white collar of his shirt.

He turned just as I reached the table. He didn't smile, didn't say anything, but in that moment, I felt that we had known each other for a long time. He stood to greet me and held the chair for me to sit. Strangely, I felt a rush of nervous energy and had to tuck my hands into my lap in case their trembling gave me away.

He didn't entirely fit the profile I had constructed. In some cases, I had given him more attractive features and had totally missed others. The hands, curved around the stem of the wine glass, I had faithfully recorded. Where we had fallen easily into conversation on the telephone, our attempts were more stilted in person.

Our respective careers provided some means of reconnecting, but I'd hoped that we would find other common ground. We were very different people – or so it seemed on that first dinner date, but rather than it being a problem, the differences were stimulating. After that dinner, I found myself reliving some of our conversations and dwelling on certain things he'd said.

Was his comment about the colour of my eyes merely an observation or something more? When our hands brushed accidently, did he feel the small electric shock, too?

I thought of the things that I had said and wondered, in retrospect, if I was too opinionated, too excited about my work. I berated myself for these thoughts, thinking that I was slipping into a submissive role, but Julian had listened intently, with that disarming smile that was warm rather than patronising. He called two days later and that annoyingly fragile part of me was relieved. But it was the more recent memories that caused me the greatest sadness; small intimacies like watching late-night movies and sharing a bowl of potato chips; deciding how to spend the rare Sundays we had together. My heart began to tighten as I reflected.

Madeleine was leaning against the retaining wall behind me, a daydream softening her gaze. Was she thinking of Carlo? Would I ever have that feeling again? It wasn't the fear of never having intimacy again that bothered me, but more the loss of Julian. I had come to count on his being there and, I admitted, had taken him for granted. When he was offered the position in London, I'd thought he wouldn't accept it, even though it was an opportunity he would never have in Australia.

"Marry me," he'd said.

I had always thought we would marry one day, but as I stared into a crumbling dessert, I suddenly felt afraid.

"You don't have to come to London," he'd answered my pause.

His proposal was heartfelt, but I was afraid our relationship might not survive the distance between us, and I didn't want him to feel obligated to me. My hesitation gave him his answer. He didn't seem surprised but stirred his macchiato mechanically, a small furrow between his eyebrows disturbing the usual tranquillity of his face. We parted amicably, though he was bruised. Again, his words as he left rang in my mind, "Be open, Dana, to the possibility of us."

I turned to my sister who was now watching me.

"Are you going to meet with Carlo?"

She hesitated before answering. "I'm not sure. I have his mobile number and the address of the hotel," she produced a slip of paper, "but... what if he didn't mean it... for me to come here with him?"

It was difficult to disguise my apprehension, but I tried, for her sake. "You could leave a message at the hotel's reception," I offered. "That way..."

"Yes!" She smiled. "That way, the ball's in his court!" Madeleine stood up and took a long sip of water as if about to take on a physical challenge. I did the same, mustering the strength for what I felt could be a very difficult day.

"Hotel Visconti," Madeleine said, holding out the note written in Carlo's surprisingly simple and elegant hand.

Though she didn't mention it, I noticed that it also read: "Come, Madeleina."

From the large leather bag that "contained her world", she

produced the Lonely Planet guide for Italy. Flicking through the pages, she scanned the hotels under each of the affordability sections.

"Look for six stars," I suggested.

She cocked an eyebrow. A few quick manouevres around the map, a skill my sister had developed to an impressive degree, and she was able to locate our position in relation to Carlo's hotel.

"This way," she said, and began pacing ahead of me as if being drawn by a thread.

The hotel was small but expensive and faced into a piazza. Glass sliding doors opened to an elegant and modern reception with a highly glossed black-marble floor. Behind a long oak desk at the furthest end was an equally elegant receptionist whose tightly knotted hair matched the gloss of the floor. Her immaculately cut uniform, also black, fitted her frame as if tailored for her and I became acutely aware of my own dishevelled appearance. I waited for a look of disdain as we approached the desk, but Mimi, as her badge announced, smiled with warmth.

"Prego?"

Madeleine lurched forward.

"I was wondering if Carlo Giorni is staying here," she faltered. "I just wanted to leave him this note."

'Augustus', I felt inclined to add but I could feel my sister's confidence draining from her as her voice trailed away.

Mimi took the sorry piece of paper from Madeleine's hand and looked from it to her and to me. She smiled but her eyes lifted from ours to a small flurry of noise behind us.

"Sì, signorina," she said, returning her gaze. "Here is Signor Giorni now."

From where I stood, I could see the blood drain from my sister's face. Madeleine was rooted to the spot, staring ahead, while I turned to the increasing noise behind us.

It was Carlo, accompanied by another man and two statuesque women. Without a glance at the two tourists standing limply at the reception desk, one with her rigid back to him, the other sizing him up as the gigolo she knew he was, Carlo ushered the others into the lift, the sound of their laughter narrowing with the closing doors.

Mimi's look was close to pity. Madeleine turned quickly and we almost collided.

"Let's go," she said through frozen lips.

She stepped it out ahead of me, but her embarrassment kept pace. At the next street corner, she stopped.

"Did you see him?" she demanded, "Did he see me?"

"He didn't see you... or me," I soothed.

Her breathing slowed. "Who was he with?"

I told her what I'd seen.

"Was he with either of the women?"

Probably both, I thought, but told her that I couldn't be certain.

"Bastard." Madeleine hitched her "life bag" on to her shoulder. "Thank God, he didn't see me."

I didn't remind her that she had left the note.

CHAPTER FOURTEEN

W e walked on through the streets of Rome, stopping now and then to marvel at another statue, another fountain. Madeleine didn't mention the incident again; instead, she seemed more tuned to the day, more resolved about something. I felt some guilt that I had suggested she leave the note and wondered if Mimi would think to discard it. If Carlo was indeed the international racing driver he claimed to be, Mimi would be very used to women leaving their calling cards.

We walked the streets until evening, both reluctant to return to our hotel room and miss the life of Rome. Over prosciutto and egg pizza in a small pizzeria, we watched the busy Roman world go by. Only that morning, we had been finalising our time in Kos. I recalled that, as the plane had tilted in its ascent, I looked down and saw the Asklepion buffered from the world on three sides by its cypress grove. I imagined that I saw Asklepios and Hippocrates there, and fancied that they turned their faces to the sky, Asklepios raising his staff and Hippocrates with his brow furrowed in concentration.

Although I had wanted to go home only two days earlier, I

was now content to spend as long as I wanted in Rome. Madeleine was in constant awe. When we filed through the Vatican, she was bewildered by its wealth. Despite my sister's travel to exotic locations, she never failed to be surprised. It was a pleasure to experience Rome through her eyes.

"Signorine," our hotel receptionist called to us before we disappeared into the lift in the late afternoon, "this was left for you," he said, holding a small silver-grey envelope between his fingers to both of us.

"Thank you." I took it from him feeling a small knot of anticipation. "It's for you," I said, handing it to Madeleine and tried not to show my disappointment, though I wasn't certain what I was expecting. She didn't open it but tucked it into the front pocket of her bag and gestured for us to take the stairs instead of the lift. She dropped the bag on the bed like an intolerable weight and headed to the bathroom to take a shower. The silver-grey envelope half slid from the bag's pocket on to the quilt, and I saw enough to know it was from Carlo.

"Mads," I called through the partly opened bathroom door, "I'm going for a walk."

"Sorry?" she turned off the tap and the metal towel ring clattered against the tiled wall.

She peered through the steam around the door. "You've just come back from a walk."

"I'll buy some water," I said, heading to the door.

"There's some in the fridge." I heard her call as it closed behind me.

I walked aimlessly for 10 minutes or so and felt very alone. I bought the water we didn't need and found my way, almost instinctively, towards the Pantheon. I remembered how excited I was the first time I had seen it – school history lessons in Mrs Roberts's class suddenly came to life and I felt that thrill again.

I entered through its portico with the inscription to Agrippa. It took my eyes a moment to adjust to the dim light inside, but I could just make out only three other people, two talking quietly in a recessed chapel and one woman standing in the centre. Though it was nearly six o'clock, there was enough light through the large central aperture to illuminate her and she was gazing at the opening – the oculus – with a fixed, almost longing expression. As I moved forward, she turned to face me.

"Dana," she whispered, and it seemed that my name lapped the walls with centrifugal force. My breath caught in my throat, and I backed toward the entrance, noticing that the other tourists were still in conversation. I turned to rush into the comforting bustle of the street. Trembling legs found their way to a stone bench far enough away to observe the woman when she left.

I waited for half an hour with my eyes glued to the doorway but saw only the two tourists leave. Two uniformed guards arrived and went inside. After a few minutes, they came out and bolted the heavy door.

"Where have you been?" Madeleine looked up from the bed, her face full of reprimand and concern.

"Just walking... it's a beautiful evening," I said, offering her a bottle of water as evidence. Behind her, a small note in bold white sat apart from its envelope, both discarded on the bed.

"So sorry I missed you... please call me..." Madeleine quoted parts of the note and then said through a rigid jaw. "I wish I hadn't left our address there. Thank goodness I didn't leave my mobile number."

The good thing about the written note, I decided, was that it provided more time for Madeleine to consider her reply. Julian had my phone number, and I had his, but it was locked in the vault of my mobile phone.

I was going to tell Madeleine about the woman in the Pantheon but now, in a hard-surfaced hotel room with my sister contemplating a real relationship, I didn't know what I thought of it.

"I suppose you don't feel like going out again?" Madeleine gathered note and envelope and tucked them into her bag. "I'm starving."

"What are you going to do about Carlo?"

"Nothing. So..." she said, swiftly changing the subject, "why did you go out earlier?"

The noise level rose at a table by the window where two women and three men were laughing at something one of them had said. Madeleine was waiting for me to answer. When I told her I thought I was "cramping her style" she laughed. "What style?" she said, and then more seriously: "I'm here with you on a holiday. We've never done this together and... it's great." There was that dangerously moist look in her eyes that prompted me to move the conversation on. Hesitantly, I told her what had happened in the Pantheon.

"Are you sure she said your name?" Madeleine's eyes were wide with excitement. "Perhaps she knows you. You know how you can run into people in the most unlikely places..." She paused and studied me for a moment. "Dee, I hate to ask you this, but she was real, wasn't she?"

It was a question I hadn't dared to ask myself. I didn't like its implication and I didn't know what to say. My sister's concern showed as she went to the counter to order coffee.

The party of five attracted my attention as their chairs scraped across the flagstone floor. The two women, one fair and the other dark, were both in their thirties and dressed in business suits. They were in animated conversation standing at the table. One of the men was at the bar talking to a waitress, the other men were chatting as they gathered their belongings. Although there was a lot of background noise, I thought that they were speaking in English. One of them bent to retrieve his satchel from the floor and when he stood up with his back to me, I recognised the erect posture and the fair hair sitting just over the collar of his shirt.

Julian!

Startled and shaking I tried to attract Madeleine's attention, but she was experimenting with the Italian language to an amused waiter.

The dark-haired woman linked her arm in his and kissed him on the cheek. His face was still turned away from me and I couldn't determine his reaction, or the level of intimacy contained within that kiss. Madeleine was returning to the table just as they were leaving. They stopped outside the window and seemed to be discussing where they would go next. Julian, his face still not clearly visible, kissed the woman on the cheek and they unlinked arms. He turned left while the other four crossed the street and headed right.

"You think you saw Julian?" Madeleine looked at me with an expression of surprise and disbelief, but before I could stop her, she was already out the door looking for him. I drank a glass of water, and my hand was trembling when the coffee came to the table.

"I didn't see him," she said, when she returned, "and the

street is relatively quiet. I saw four people on the other side of the road, but he wasn't with them."

"He might have turned into a lane," I said, dismally.

"No," she said quickly, "the next lane is a good 50 metres away. I think you were mistaken."

I was certain it was Julian, but I no longer had the energy to argue. I sipped my coffee.

"Why don't you call him?" Madeleine said, "then we can be sure."

And what if he is in Rome? I thought. What business was it of mine? If he didn't want to meet, the conversation would be awkward; if he did, I didn't think I could slip into the role as a "friend".

Madeleine didn't persist. She stirred her coffee in silence. I turned my head to the window, not able to bear the expression on her face.

Although we had drunk a bottle of wine between us, it didn't help me sleep and I spent the night staring at the ceiling.

CHAPTER FIFTEEN

I was grateful to get up when the sun strained through the broken slit of the wooden Venetian blinds. Madeleine still hadn't stirred after I had taken a shower and was ready for the day.

"My head is killing me," she groaned her voice sounding thick beneath the blankets.

"You go... I just want to...." Her voice trailed off as she fell back into sleep.

I placed water and her phone on the bedside table and left.

Outside, the streets were frenetic with commuters and, as I stepped on to the pavement, I imagined what it would be like to set off to work at a Roman hospital. I eyed the apartments a few doors down and, as I passed, two women dressed for the office came through the gate and paused to talk. The gate was left open, and I could just make out the large foyer with its polished concrete floor, glass walls and metal finishes. I imagined myself returning there after a day at the hospital, living as a Roman and briefly entertained the idea of applying for a position – there was little left for me in Melbourne. But the thought filled me with fear. There were other possibilities of work open to me, but they would always be second best to what I loved, had loved, the most.

In a secluded piazza, I breakfasted on fruit and coffee and scanned a newspaper, testing my rudimentary knowledge of Italian. Political news dominated the front page; a starlet's ordinary moment stolen by the paparazzi's flash on page three; below her startled gaze, a smaller article and photo of one man flanked by three Nordic beauties. The man... Carlo Augustus Giorni. I could understand enough of the article to know that it mentioned his return, an injury and the cloud over his fitness for a race. The girls it seemed, did not rate a mention. Carlo wore women as women might wear costume jewellery.

I thought of my sister tucked up in bed with her headache and squeezed my way through the patrons drinking coffee at the bar to pay my bill. When I returned to the hotel with paracetamol, Madeleine was deep in sleep. Her forehead radiated a normal heat and her breathing was deep and slow.

While she slept, I wrote to our parents. They were of the generation who still valued the written letter – something to store with all the other mementoes of life.

What would I think of the contents of this letter if I were to read it in 10 or even 20 years' time? Where would I be in my life?

The future seemed to be a gaping abyss. At the thought that my parents might not be alive in 20 years, I wrote with a greater intensity. Correspondence so far had been notes on postcards and occasional telephone calls.

My mother would pass the letter to my father and ask him to read my "news". It was strange that she was the keeper of the memorabilia and wondered if she was stockpiling evidence of happy childhoods and, therefore, successful mothering. Madeleine was kinder in her reflections on our childhood though she had the perspective of the younger child; our mother had gained more experience and had warmed to her role a little more the second time around.

Our parents were an odd union, opposites in both the obvious and the fundamental ways. Yet, it worked, or at least it had lasted. In its way, their relationship became the benchmark for my own, but Julian and I, opposites in the obvious, and so similar in the fundamentals, could not survive.

Madeleine slept on and didn't stir when I leant over her to tell her I was going out. I wrote a note and left it on the bedside table.

The post office was easy to find and, after I had sent my letter on its journey home, I found myself walking again in the direction of the Pantheon. Inside was full of tourists, pausing at different points around the walls and whispering to each other. This morning, only dull sunlight filtered through the oculus and cast a weak glow on the western wall.

I looked among the tourists for the woman, though I doubted that I would find her there. Reconstructing the scene in my mind gave no more weight to its reality and I was about to leave when I noticed a doorway on the eastern wall that was almost obscured by a colonnade. When I pushed, it opened smoothly, and I found myself standing in a piazza dominated by Bernini's elephant and obelisk.

Cars were parked at haphazard angles around a large church and the piazza was busy with people going about their day. Usually, in such a crowd, I would feel anonymous, but I had the feeling that I was being watched. On the other side of the square, standing on the steps of the church, was the woman I had seen the day earlier. When she knew that I'd seen her, she entered. I ran towards the steps, weaving through parked cars and almost colliding with a group of men parting after a conversation.

"Ahhh signorina... Bella!" I heard them laugh.

I ran up the seven steps and through the open doors. The silence inside hit me like a soft punch and it took me a moment to adjust to the blood-filled light as the morning sun streamed through the ruby stained-glass windows. From the entrance, I couldn't see the woman and I explored the recesses and side chapels. The stranger was nowhere to be seen.

As I passed the altar, I paused to dip my head, a legacy of my Catholic education. It had been a long time since I had worshipped in a church, and I sat down in a wooden pew bowed and bleached by centuries of pious backsides.

When I was young, I had spent a great deal of time in the local church. I was a member of the choir, of the Children of Mary, and I would never miss Sunday mass. My devotion and discipline were self-inflicted. My father, though baptised in the Catholic Church, was an atheist. My mother dipped in and out of her Anglican faith, depending on her social engagements. She was bemused by her devout daughter, and I relished that fact. That my Protestant mother might not go to heaven was a strange comfort to me and I adopted, in matters of faith at least, a sanctimonious air.

When she was old enough, Madeleine came with me to church. Perhaps it was my rigour that turned her off, but Madeleine was never comfortable with Catholicism. For years, she shopped around the eastern religions, but eventually gave them away to devote herself to her gardens. It took me longer to leave but I hadn't noticed that my spiritual life was diminishing. When its formal expression petered out, I didn't feel the need to replace it. I had worn my faith like a mantle, and I simply replaced it with my work.

As I sat in the silence of that church, I longed for the simple faith that I had lost. I would never again have an unquestioning belief, but I wanted that feeling of connection to something more than my own experiences. I'd had that in my work, especially bringing new life into the world.

When I returned to the hotel, Madeleine had showered and was wearing a feminine floral dress. Though her eyes were darkly shadowed against her pale face, she looked beautiful.

"Carlo rang," she said, and although her tone suggested, "and he's wasting his time," there was a sparkle in her dark eyes. "He wants me to meet him for lunch."

I remembered the newspaper article, but it was too late to mention it.

"Where are you meeting him?"

"Actually," she began, the colour rising in her cheeks, "he's sending a car to pick me up. Is that all right? Will you be OK?"

Madeleine's need for reassurance was not lost on me and I felt guilty.

"Of course," I said. "There's plenty to see."

Madeleine looked at me seriously, "Perhaps I should cancel... I want to sightsee with you."

"Well," I said, picking a speck of lint from her dress, "to be honest, I wouldn't mind a day just pottering around in my own thoughts."

She brightened and inspected herself in the mirror. The telephone on the bedside table rang. "The car's here," she said, placing the receiver down as if it was made of fine porcelain. She picked up her bag and we walked to the door together.

"Have a great day." I felt as if I was sending my daughter off on a first date. The trouble was that I couldn't ban her from seeing Carlo, though I truly wished I could.

After she left, I looked around the small room, but there was nothing to keep me there. If I was home in Melbourne, I would have caught up on reading – medical journals, usually. It had been a long time since I'd read a novel to its end, often falling asleep mid-sentence.

On the rare days off work, I would attempt to bring order to the unruly growth in my small courtyard. Mostly, the plants were in pots, even though I had lived in my townhouse for five years. Sometimes, Madeleine would come to rescue them. She had wonderful ideas for my courtyard and, after Julian had left, had surprised me by setting up a small rectangular oasis, complete with table and chairs and tubs of fragrant kitchen herbs. At least they have a practical use, she had said with a smile. It had proved to be a wonderful gift. I hadn't anticipated sitting among those plants very often and worried they would reveal my neglect before too long. After Bonnie's death, they became like intimate friends and my eyes became attuned to their needs and deviations in their health.

I sat on the bed and studied tourist brochures we had collected. There were still so many places to explore in the city, so I traced a route, collected a water from the bar fridge and stepped out again into the street.

CHAPTER SIXTEEN

The sun was high in the sky and its heat was a reminder of the imminent summer, the summer I was chasing. Abandoning the planned route, I headed instead towards the river. On my way, I found myself veering into the Via Frattina where I thought I had seen Julian the previous night.

The cafés were already crowding and reminded me of the early-morning bustle in the city lanes of Melbourne. Occasionally, before a midmorning appointment with a patient, I would eat breakfast at a window table and watch the commuters pour from the subterranean world of Flinders Street Station through the gaping exit into Degraves Street. There were stories drifting in that flow – of love and grief, of joy and depression. After Bonnie, I continued to go there for a while, wishing that I could be caught in their slipstream.

In the Via Frattina, I felt as if I was walking on eggs and that I was watching myself like a stranger. I didn't know what I thought I would find, but I'd been convinced that it was Julian I had seen the previous night. The table for five in the window of the café had been separated into two smaller ones. Two men at one table were in deep conversation but paused to give me appreciative looks as I glanced in.

I walked with a stiffened nonchalance in the direction that Julian had taken. No side streets for 50 metres, Madeleine had said, but only 20 or so metres on, a narrow access she must have missed sliced through to the street beyond. I turned into it.

Large rubbish bins lined the lane that was only wide enough for a single truck. Several people passed through, using the short cut to the Via della Vite. I paused at the end of the lane, having no idea which way Julian might have gone, and turned right to take up a route to the River Tiber.

I passed a bewildering number of hotels and, by the time I came to the river, I gave up any idea of finding him. I walked along the river's banks as I had done many times along the Yarra River at home. The differences between the two cities should have been apparent, but, from my perspective, it all seemed the same – other people's lives breathing at my back.

Along the cobbled path, people walked or cycled together. To my right, the She-wolf had been etched into the high flood walls, her head lowered to be stroked. She looked out benignly, despite the graffiti of male genitalia that had been spray-painted beneath her full teats.

Conversation drifted around me like a fog until I heard a familiar voice that pierced the air. I felt my heart and mind pause to take it in. I turned quickly to those walking behind me, but already the voice was becoming distant and blurred. Ahead, a couple was walking deep in conversation. The man was talking, his head bowed as though discussing something of great importance. The woman at his side was listening with full and intense concentration, her head tilted slightly towards him. She was the blonde woman who had been at Julian's table the previous night and now, as I walked behind them, the breadth of the man's back and lean of his left shoulder convinced me that it was indeed Julian.

They were far enough from me that I could follow without being seen. Several times, I lost sight of them, and I heard the tut of tongues as I pushed past an ambling couple in order to make some ground. At the Ponte Fabricio they turned and crossed to Tiber Island and were lost to me briefly as they merged with pedestrians crossing the bridge in both directions.

Once on the island, most turned right but Julian and the woman descended the steps towards the river on the other side. I followed them through narrow alleys and steps and twice they paused and faced each other to discuss some matter. I froze on my spot. In that time as I followed, the most I saw of Julian's face was his profile, as I had the night before. From a distance, he looked thinner and seemed to be troubled. The woman occasionally reached out to touch his arm, though, beyond this, they didn't seem to share any deeper intimacy.

I followed them down the steps to the lower levels of the island that sat 10 metres above the swirling grey of the Tiber River. As they turned to the right, a tour group overtook me and formed a barrier between us. When they dispersed, I had lost sight of them completely.

Dejected, I returned to the steps, disturbed by what I was becoming. In simple terms, I was stalking Julian. Halfway up the steps I paused, wondering what to do next. My eyes wandered along the alluvial foundation that supported the basilica above. Etched into the weathered layers was the outline of a ship and, beneath it, a carved snake extended the ship's length. Asklepios, I remembered in Ovid's story, had saved this city from plague. A great yearning came over me then and, with my back to the rock face, I sat on a step huddled to the rail.

Coolness seeped into the base of my spine, and I shuffled, checking the steps for dampness. It began to rise into the pit of my back and to work its way up my spine like the slow creep of mercury in an old-fashioned thermometer. I raised my arms and flexed my back, blaming foreign mattresses and long air flights, but it continued and, as it rose into the base of my skull, I began to panic, wondering if I'd contracted a meningeal infection. The moment I closed my eyes there was a silent explosion of light that was both wondrous and fearsome. I felt, in that moment, my body had no boundaries and no substance. When I opened my eyes, nothing had changed. The sensation left me, but I felt a strange lightness as though something physical or mental had been shed.

I got up and continued up the steps to the promenade. There were a few people strolling along the travertine, but I didn't see Julian among them. At the western end of the island stood a two-storey sandstone building surrounded by large cypress trees. Along the path leading to it, a sign read Fatebene-fratelli Hospital.

The entrance to the hospital was recessed into the side of the building. Sliding doors opened as I approached. Though I hadn't thought to go in, I was now intrigued and turned off my phone before entering. The reception area was welcoming with the gentle lighting of wall lamps rather than harsh fluorescents, though the kindness of the light couldn't disguise the cracks in the walls' plaster and the small chips in the marble floor.

There was no one at the reception desk and I read what I could understand on the bulletins pinned to the blue felt notice board to my right. In one section, there were photographs of what seemed to be a farewell party. One elderly man featured in many of the photographs, always seated centrally with a different group of people. In one of these, a group of about 10 was huddled around him and beaming for the camera. I scanned the faces and one caught my eye. She was standing to his right and bending forward, her hands resting on his shoulders. There was something about the way her head was angled, the loose, fair curls that brushed her face and the intensity of her gaze into the camera. I was certain she was the woman in the Pantheon.

I turned away in shock, feeling all the while her gaze lingering on my back. Across the room, the names of the doctors and their specialties were listed in alphabetical order. The hospital housed a range of specialists in urology, neurology and obstetrics, an odd collection in an equally odd location on this island. Among the 12 or so names I noticed there were only two women.

A voice from behind jolted me. A severe-looking woman in middle-age was placing her handbag behind the reception desk and moved, with a stiff hip, towards me. I backed away from the board and eased my way to the photograph on the other side; she followed. I pointed to the woman in the photograph.

"I'm looking for..." I raised my eyes as if trying to recall a name. "Dottoressa...?"

The woman's shrewd eyes took me in.

"Dottoressa Lorenzo," she told me, then asked slowly in thickly accented English: "And your name?" She gestured back to the desk where, it seemed, our conversation was to resume.

"Dana... Doctor Dana Cavanagh."

As her arthritic fingers pencilled my name – though I noted she didn't ask for its spelling – I pondered that of the woman in the photograph. I did know it and had read a paper by her at some time in the months before Bonnie's death.

"The dottoressa is not here." She looked up with a forced smile. "She is in London for three weeks."

Feeling as if I had been dismissed, I left the reception and returned to the path along the travertine. Dottoressa Lorenzo was the hospital's obstetrician.

———

When I returned to the hotel, there was a phone message waiting for me at reception. "Carlo has invited us for dinner. Car will pick you up at seven. Love M. PS Turn on your phone!"

The last thing I wanted was to sit in dining proximity to Carlo Giorni, but there was no arguing with this note. With an hour to go, I showered, dressed and sat with my cup of tea by the window, watching the Roman world go by. I might have been in a bustling European city, but I felt like the loneliest person in the world.

I looked over to Madeleine's bed; her bits and pieces were scattered around the room – a hairbrush that had captured long strands of her hair, a lean make-up bag, and a packet of mints with curled paper where she had torn it open. It seemed that she, too, had left me.

CHAPTER SEVENTEEN

T he car arrived on the hour. The driver, a portly man with a beatific face, opened the door with a flourish. Though the Peugeot was an older model, the leather upholstery inside was still richly coloured and pliable and the highly polished dashboard reflected loving care.

Gaetano, as my driver introduced himself, drove beyond the centre of the city, passing suburbs of old concrete and new apartments, supermarkets and petrol stations until the historic precinct seemed to be only a dream.

Twenty minutes later, we climbed into the southern hills so richly green in contrast to the grey of the suburbs. We passed villas on large estates often surrounded by their own small forests – some ostentatious, some elegant and stately. We turned off the road and paused before massive wrought-iron gates that opened slowly as we crept closer. At the end of a long bitumen drive lined with chestnut trees, a three-storey villa of dusky-pink stucco was angled away from the drive.

As the car swung in a graceful curve in front of the steps leading to the house, my sister appeared at the oak double front doors. When she saw me in the back of the car, she waved excitedly. It felt, suddenly, that I had been transported to a future time, with Madeleine greeting me to her home. I imagined children running to join her on the verandah to greet their foreign aunt. Instead, Carlo appeared behind her. He rested one hand on her shoulder and, with the other swept the air in a gesture meant to be of greeting, but there was something disconcerting about his stance, his ownership of Madeleine. Was the elegant gesture one of warning? I waved back.

"Dee," Madeleine whispered excitedly as she came forward and opened the door, "isn't this place unbelievable!"

"Buongiorno, Dana." Carlo's smooth voice seeped between her mouth and my ear.

Never good at hiding my feelings, I tried, for my sister's sake. "Carlo," I responded, extending my hand in greeting and the long fingers that had beckoned me in my dream clasped mine.

When I climbed the steps to the balcony, I gasped with pleasure. Behind the villa was a vast darkness and, halfway to the horizon, a line of lights defined the edge to Lake Albano.

The entrance to the villa was expansive. Marble, glass and wrought iron worked to produce a look of restrained opulence, so different from the effect of the mock villas I had seen in some outer suburbs of Melbourne. A staircase took up the central position and flared on to the floor of the entrance. Double doors opened to large rooms – a sitting room on the left and a dining room on the right. Madeleine, walking ahead of me, turned to see my reaction. She was radiant. The colour had returned to her face and the shadows beneath her eyes had lightened. She had paused in front of a large vase of flowers that matched her dress exactly. I smiled in genuine appreciation of all that was beautiful before me.

As Carlo ushered us into the dining room, I noticed he was

still unable to put pressure on his right foot. Madeleine's fine heels made a soft, feminine tap on the marble floor as she walked while the heavier rubber of my practical heels made no sound. A long dining room table that would comfortably sit 20 was the centrepiece of the room, though it appeared much larger in an enormous mirror on the far wall. I wondered what this suggested about Carlo and the number of people he could call friends. This table, I noted, was not set for us, instead, at the furthest end of the room, a smaller one in front of French doors was set for four. A candelabra at its centre gave a soft light that danced in the crystal of the glasses and refracted into coloured beams on to the cutlery. The effect was enchanting, and I wondered if Carlo had the capacity to control the elements.

"Dana." Carlo spoke. "We are so pleased you come."

We? I shot a look at Madeleine. She smiled in agreement, but her eyes darted from Carlo to me and back again.

"You have a beautiful home." I forced a half-hearted smile to my own lips.

"Dee," Madeleine asked, her voice soothing, "what did you do this afternoon?"

When I related the events of the day, a stripped version – a walk along the Tiber, a visit to the hospital – I could almost believe that the day had unfolded in such a benign way. The other – Julian, the woman in the photograph – seemed too fanciful in this gentle light and solidity. My account was made duller by a sudden wave of fatigue that swept over me and I was grateful to be interrupted by the arrival of an elegant older woman. Carlo rested the ringed hand on the woman's arm as she placed a covered dish on the table.

"Mama... Sophia ... this is Dana, sister of Madeleina."

Carlo's mother looked confused, and he repeated in Italian.

"Ah... Sì..." Signora Giorni moved towards me. I rose

unsteadily from my chair to greet her and extended my hand. Hers was cool, but warmth was held in the deep brown eyes that looked as though they were a portal for life's pain and joy.

"Dana," she repeated my name, her gentle voice soothing me back into my seat. Her hands moved to my arm as she turned to Carlo. Her voice was soft, but sad as she spoke to him in their tongue. He nodded, looking almost grave, but changed the tone of conversation between them quickly.

"Sophia thinks you look tired, Dana," he said with a smile. "But she is... you know... a mother. She tells me this all the time."

"You do look tired, Dee. Are you OK?" Madeleine leaned towards me.

As I focussed on the three faces watching me, I felt suddenly unable to speak, as if I was again trapped in the membranous room of my dream. This time the hand, those fingers penetrated through the wall and grabbed me by the shoulder.

I was aware then of being supported in caring arms, of being guided up the staircase to a bed and Madeleine's voice trying to calm me, though I could also hear her distress. Only Sophia's face brought me comfort. Her eyes penetrated as if able to see to the core of me. Over and over, she whispered my name and, from her lips that name seemed to resonate with promise. I strained to hear it.

When I woke, the room glowed with the warmth of golden light from the lamp on the bedside table. I was in a single bed with its twin on the other side of the room. Madeleine's "life bag" blossomed in the green and gold leaves of the bedspread. Though my head was still foggy, I felt much better. The lamplight was too dull to read the time on my watch, so I made my way, tentatively, across the room to the window. Outside, that same moon that had cast a cold and accusing beam into my bedroom at home, lit, in monotone, some sections of the Giorni estate. The rest lay deeply in shadow.

I crossed the floor to the bedroom door and heard the low murmurs of conversation below. My hand, sliding along the banister, guided me down the stairs. To the right, one of the doors to the sitting room was ajar. Inside, Sophia sat on a leather sofa. Though they were obscured by the door I could hear Madeleine and Carlo talking opposite her, and Sophia would nod her head as Carlo translated. The room glowed with the light from an enormous fireplace between them at the back of the room. It was a comfortable family scene. In the comparative vacancy of the entrance, I shivered with cold and returned upstairs.

CHAPTER EIGHTEEN

The next morning, when I woke to my sister's form in the other bed, I was disoriented. We had slept in parallel for weeks and bedrooms were beginning to fuse into each other. I was feeling stronger and now the events of the previous evening seemed like a dream. I got up, slipped on my skirt and jumper that I'd laid over a nearby chair and crept out the door. The sounds of pots, cutlery and the smell of freshly baked bread and salty fried meat met me at the bottom of the stairs.

In the dining room, the large table was set for four at one end. The smaller table from the previous night had been removed and I stood in the space created trying to recall what had led me to collapse. The French doors opened on to a chaotic and enchanting herb garden flanked by another section of the villa set at right angles and I stepped out on to the flagstone paving.

Outside, the courtyard garden glistened with dew in the morning sun, and I looked among the herbs for those I recognised. Though it was too early for their scent, I imagined I could smell them. At home, I would run my hands through the lavender, the rosemary and the lemon thyme and inhale that heady mix deeply. In this courtyard, I found some favourites but there were many I didn't know. I picked a leaf of one and rubbed it between my fingers.

"For heart."

The voice startled me, and I turned quickly. Sophia was coming out of the kitchen. As she came towards me, she stopped at a garden bed and picked a few leaves from a plant I couldn't see. She straightened without effort and the morning sun, now perched on the garden wall, shone on to her face. For the briefest of moments, she resembled the woman in the Pantheon. I remembered the way that face captured the light, just as Sophia's did now. The similarity disappeared quickly, and I scolded myself for what seemed like the beginning of an obsession.

"Come, Dana." She turned away and gestured for me to follow her to a garden bench. Obediently, I joined her, and we sat in companionable silence.

"It's beautiful, Sophia," I said at last.

"Bello..." Her affirmation extended into a long sigh of satisfaction. Again, we sat in silence. When I turned to Sophia to speak, the morning light had ignited her hair so that even the grey held that light to itself. When she turned to me, I saw that her eyes were not the deep unfathomable brown I had thought, but were more like the shallow riverbeds of Australia, tannin-stained from fallen river gums. She waited for me to speak, but suddenly, I found I had nothing to say. All that was needed was held in that moment. I swallowed against the small choking sensation in my throat. Sophia patted my hand and turned her face to the garden again.

For 20 minutes or more we sat together. Occasionally, she would get up from the bench and tend to the needs of her garden – pruning wilting leaves, clicking her tongue over a broken stalk. At one point she began talking quickly in a scolding voice that took me by surprise, but at her feet emerged a beautiful tortoiseshell cat that responded to her reprimand by curling its long body around her thin ankles.

When she disappeared into the kitchen with the cat following languidly behind her, I wandered around the garden beds looking for a traditional design under the chaos. Certainly, bay trees were centre points, but the growth was so dense it was difficult to determine if they conformed to a pattern. The paths meandered without obvious purpose, other than to surprise the wanderer with dead ends that drew the eye to a tiny flower of exquisite design, to a hairy leaf that beckoned to be stroked or, in one, the shards of an urn of indeterminate age. I thought of the pseudo-relics sold in nurseries at home to bring that "authentic Italian touch" to Melbourne backyards.

The cat, lying in the doorway to the kitchen looked at Sophia with bewilderment as she stepped over it and came towards me with a steaming cup and saucer in one hand.

"Camomilla," she said, offering it to me.

The tea was honey-coloured and fragrant and small white petals bobbed in its swirls. With the cup in one hand, I turned towards a sundial that was just visible through the fennel stalks. Sophia shrugged her shoulders as though time was irrelevant to her, then, as if to make some point, she tapped my arm and bent down to the plants at her feet. In that section, yellowing parsley leaves dominated. She tugged at them until she had cleared a patch and then beckoned me to look closer. Small parsley shoots were now exposed to the light.

She left me then to drink my tea in the morning sun. The cat, forgiving the stranger who had taken away the attention, wove a knot around my ankles that bound me to that garden. Madeleine found me there an hour later.

"I'm fine, "I said before she could ask. "Just too tired, I think."

"Carlo will call his doctor," she said.

"He won't!" The words escaped my lips before I could think.

Madeleine's lids closed slowly as if shutting me out for that moment.

"Mads." I reached for her hand. "I've just got a heavy period."

She looked at me with mild surprise but gave a small shrug of acceptance.

"OK," she said, standing up, "I'll tell Carlo not to call. Breakfast is ready in the dining room."

"I'll be there in a minute."

My reluctance to leave the peace of the garden was heightened by the trail of annoyance that drifted behind my sister.

When I entered the dining room, only Sophia looked up to greet me. She slid her small frame around the table and came to me with her long, elegant fingers outstretched. She all but lowered me into a chair, placed the napkin on my lap and patted my hair. There was such warmth in that touch. I thought of my mother tucking me into bed when I was a child. She would make an inordinate fuss of the folding back of the blanket, the sheet folded out so that the embroidered rabbits faced anyone who might come into the room. When satisfied with the effect she would pat my hair and kiss my cheek as if I were the dot on the "i" or the stroke across the "t".

"Buongiorno, Dana." Carlo's voice slicked across the moment. "You are feeling better?"

"I am, thank you."

He held my gaze. Madeleine was silent over her sautéed mushrooms.

"Today, Dana," he continued, "I have time trial. I ask Madeleina to come with me. She would like you to join us."

Was Carlo now speaking for my sister? I could feel anger giving me back the colour I'd lost the night before. As if reading my mind, she looked up. "Dee, will you come? If you feel well enough."

"I don't think I'm up to it, Mads, "I said, truthfully. My blood pressure began a slow descent at the thought of whining engines and inflated egos. "I'll go back to the hotel and rest, I think."

She looked at Carlo with concern. "I'll go with Dana. She's not well enough."

Sophia spoke rapidly to her son.

"My mother invite you to stay here today, Dana."

I saw the smallest expression of hope on my sister's face. My day was decided.

In the bedroom, Madeleine tried to change my mind. She felt guilty, she said, because I had been ill, because we were on holidays together and, although she didn't say it, because she was in love.

I tried to assure her I was happy to spend the day at the villa, but she was unconvinced and left with Carlo less excited than she had been. It was my turn to feel guilty and I wondered about my own motives. I wanted my sister to be happy; I just didn't think it would be possible with Carlo.

CHAPTER NINETEEN

After they had gone, I decided to walk to the lake. Sweet sounds of someone humming met me at the base of the staircase and I paused to listen. I thought of my aunt who would trill her favourite songs while teaching me how to cook. Winter Saturdays were spent in her kitchen while our parents and uncle went to the football. We would prepare sausage, baked beans and pineapple casserole, Lamingtons made from stale sponge cake dipped in melted chocolate and coconut, all served in crystal dishes on a lace-dressed dining table. After dinner, we would watch the football replay and toast crumpets over the gas heater. Though I had dismissed this life as trivial, it now seemed simply wonderful in its simplicity.

The hum led me to the kitchen I'd seen from the garden. It was a huge room that combined the best of country wood and modern stainless steel. At a central bench was a large woman kneading dough. As she thumped and turned the dough over, a puff of flour enveloped her. Her red face formed a nucleus in a white electron cloud. When she saw me in the doorway, she acknowledged me with a lift of her eyebrows and indicated, with a dart of her eyes, the stool on the other side of the bench.

Discreetly, I sat down and watched. Beside her were small poaching rings and I had an almost irresistible urge to press one deep into the dough. As if reading my mind, she paused and gestured to the rings with powdered fingers. I laughed with surprise and leaned out of my chair, picking one up and hesitating in case I had misunderstood.

The Nucleus waited.

"Scones?" I was perplexed.

She shrugged her shoulders.

"Sì... sì..." she insisted and nodded her head.

Slowly, I pressed the ring into the pillow of dough and gave a slight turn as my aunt had taught me. If I'd closed my eyes, I would have been back in her kitchen, the football on the radio, the silverside roasting with onions and cloves, the hydrangea tapping at the window demanding to be pruned, and the table covered in tiny, buttered flour balls.

"Sì," the Nucleus said, and nodded for me to continue while she turned to her steaming pot on the stove. I pressed on, placing the scones on the greased tray beside the bowl, and rolled the scraps into a ball to eke out another one or two. While the Nucleus still had her back to me, I shaped the remaining slivers into two tiny leaves and scoured their edges with a knife. With my aunt's care, I placed them on one of the misshapen scones and rolled a tiny flower to place in the middle.

When she returned to the bench the Nucleus laughed at the sight of my little creation.

"Bella," she said, with full approval.

The tray was whisked into the oven and the bench wiped down. I waited but she smiled and continued to clean. When she took off her apron and primped her hair her electron cloud disappeared. Without it she was a middle-aged woman with high blood pressure.

Don't leave the scones too long, I wanted to tell her, feeling a sudden protectiveness and expertise in cooking English fare. Would there be jam? And cream? Would she brew real tea and remember to take the pot to the kettle?

I looked around for the kettle but there was only a tap in the wall.

From my stool, there was a different perspective of the herb garden; it was more regularly shaped than I had thought. On the northern wall was a door I hadn't noticed earlier, but its flaking paint and exposed wood were a perfect camouflage. The door's condition was incongruous in this immaculately maintained villa but seemed to be an acknowledgement of the garden's rampant and chaotic beauty. I sat and took it in, content to allow time to pass slowly.

Eventually, the Nucleus removed the scones from the oven and tipped them on to a cooling rack. I despaired for my little floral creation, but, with heat-hardened fingers she placed it delicately on a plate. Chuckling, she waved it under my eyes for approval and whisked it away. Later, I assumed, I would eat my scone.

I opened the kitchen door to the garden. Outside was warmer than an hour earlier and, as the dew dried on the plants the more potent herbs gave off a heady scent. Only the bed in front of the old door still lay in shadow. I looked back to see if the Nucleus was watching and when I couldn't see her, I stepped carefully through the bed.

The door's handle had long gone. I pushed at the brittle wood, but it had swollen into a stubborn position. I moved closer and leaned my weight behind my shoulder. The door gave a small squeak of fright. I hesitated and scanned the upstairs windows and the dining room in case Sophia had seen me, but I was compelled to continue. I pushed harder and the door gave a warped groan of disapproval, finally swinging away from the frame.

I stepped out. A flagstone tilted in the soft soil as I rested my weight. Stones led away from the door toward the lake. I pulled the door behind me. Ahead, Lake Alberto glittered in the morning light, and I had to shade my eyes. To my left was an orchard where buds were already swelling on arthritic limbs. The track to the lake forked with one prong continuing ahead, while the other led to a forest on my right.

I paused, intending to continue to the lake when something caught my right peripheral vision. A bird? I turned to look but it had gone. I resumed my walk, but again there was a movement like the flap of large wings. I turned quickly and I saw a woman standing on the path that met the forest, her dress swaying lightly in the breeze. She turned in towards the trees and I ran along the path to follow.

At the edge of the forest I hesitated, then entered. The trees, birch and elm, were not as dense as I'd first thought, but they formed a shade overhead that dimmed the morning light. I followed a path barely visible under the detritus of fallen leaves. The woman had disappeared, but I was no longer surprised by her strobing appearances.

The forest thinned out into woodland and the light that filtered through was tinted with the lime green of new growth. The track had reinvented itself paved with large flat stones that were laid at irregular angles. I stepped from one to the other and realised I was avoiding the cracks between in a childhood game – Madeleine would push me from behind, frustrated that she inevitably failed and that I never did. Still, there was no sign of the woman and I had to acknowledge that she might not exist at all. For the moment, I was at peace and, while I was aware of the dangers of wandering through the woods on my own, I was unafraid; I didn't care, and I felt comfort and strength in my apathy.

The woods twittered. I stopped to listen to unfamiliar bird calls and had to dip my head as a pair of robins flew past my head in a sexual chase. I thought of Carlo now speeding around the circuit under my sister's adoring gaze. A small rustle in the leaf litter drew me into the trees. A robin bobbed between the mouldering leaves and raised a fat-bodied worm in its beak. As I tiptoed closer it swallowed the worm whole and ran a few paces ahead, looking for more. For several metres, I followed until it gave up and flew away with an irritated flutter.

I'd gone further from the path than I'd thought. When I turned a full circle, I saw that I was standing in a small glade with a floor of winter's debris – a variety of leaves melded into a single mass of humus. Where the sun struck the ground, thin tufts of steam rose and the smell reminded me of the organic scent of birth.

Kneeling in that carpet, I brought a lump of humus to my nose. I closed my eyes and drank in its scent and saw myself coaxing a slippery infant into the world. I heard the suck as it took a life's dive into my hands and then, the smell of mucous and blood as the placenta was expelled to its death. I shook my head to rattle and disassemble the thoughts that were forming.

As I returned the soil to the ground something glinted as my hand brushed aside leaves. A child's marble. I picked it up and rolled it in my palm, remembering games played on the Westminster carpet while the Sunday roast hissed and spat in the oven. Madeleine was the marble champion. She had an eye for straight lines that I recognised in the ordered chaos of her gardens. She loved winning those games and I would grow tense when, as the winner, she had the right to claim any of my marbles. There was only one I had possessed greedily – a small glaucoma-ed blue eye. She never asked for it. The one in my hand was a brown cat's eye and I recalled the family myth that if you stared into it, it would see into your soul. I'd been too afraid to look when I was young, believing that my soul belonged to God. I didn't have that concern now and held the marble to the light.

I closed my eyes and allowed my mind to empty. Disjointed images flicked by – faces I didn't recognise one after the other, as if in a procession. And again, there was the smell of fish and soil and sun-warmed fruit that had first come to me at the Asklepion. I watched as the aged and the sick were guided into the waters of a deep spring and felt that I was standing on the opposite bank, beneath a great oak tree, beckoning them to me.

The chill of the damp soil crept into my knees. I opened my eyes to find that the sun had dipped behind clouds that were thickening to form a menace. The small glade was silent and seemed to have lost its innocence. I put the marble in my pocket and found my way back to the pathway.

CHAPTER TWENTY

W hen I returned to the villa, through the front door,
Sophia was coming down the staircase. She greeted
me with arms outstretched and embraced me with great tender-
ness. She ran the back of her hand down the side of my face
smiling with satisfaction.

"The air," she said, circling the space between us, "is good."

She led me through the dining room to the kitchen.

"Per favore," she said, seating me on the stool where I had
watched the Nucleus perform.

From a heavy oak cupboard, she lifted down a silver teapot
so polished that light bounced from its surface and danced in
small silver and green circles on the walls and floor. She
measured tea leaves from an alabaster jar and half-filled the
teapot, not from the tap in the urn, but from a steaming cast-
iron kettle on the stove. She turned the pot, three times to the
right, three to the left and went into the dining room. Again, I
thought of my aunt in her kitchen and the ritual of tea-making.
I thought, too, of my own silver teapot tarnishing behind plastic
containers in my kitchen cupboard.

Sophia returned with two exquisite cups and saucers – fine white china as fragile as a baby's skull. From a covered baking tray near the stove, she produced my little scone and placed it in front of me. Her lips smiled as she put it down and then she brought jam and cream from the refrigerator. She returned with the teapot and placed it, knife and a porcelain strainer in front of me. In all this time Sophia had not spoken and I began to feel that I was partaking in a religious rite. Finally, she sat down opposite me.

"Prego, Dana," she said, nodding toward the teapot.

I poured slowly, my hand almost shaking with the weight of the occasion.

Over that perfect Devonshire tea in a Roman villa, I told Sophia about my life, about Julian, my work and the event that changed everything. I talked on and on, though I don't know how much she understood, but she nodded and smiled and when I wept, she clasped my hand. We had drunk the full pot of tea in the space of an hour. My little scone sat patiently on its plate and when I finished talking, I ate it as though I had been energised. Sophia brought me another.

When I reached into my pocket looking for a tissue, the marble beat against my hand. I took it out and showed it to her, telling her the family myth. She took it from me and held it to the light but shrugged her shoulders. She gave it back and took my empty cup instead. Inside its rim was peppered with the fine tea leaves. Sophia placed it upside down on the bench and rotated it. The glasses hanging from her neck on a fine gold chain were brought to her eyes and she studied the dregs, her face alternating between light frowns of concentration and of peace.

"A place, Dana... close to your..." She touched her chest as she struggled with the English and looked at me over the top of her spectacles. "Old place... water... and a woman who calls you." That was all. Sophia removed her glasses and placed the cup on the table. She watched me with patient expectation.

I didn't know what to say.

"Perhaps my mother is missing me," I offered but, when I said it, I thought of the woman who now dipped in and out of my reality.

"Sì... sì," Sophia nodded in understanding as she stood up and took the cups and saucers to the sink. She turned back to me, "You like a – how d'you say? – bath?"

I nodded, feeling briefly as though she were my mother and I had just returned home from primary school.

Sophia left me at the bench. I could hear her talking in rapid Italian and when she returned, she gestured for me to follow her. On the landing of the first level a young woman dressed in the black and white of a domestic servant was carrying a folded white towel and robe to the bathroom. Sophia gave her a few short instructions and the woman nodded. When she opened the bathroom door, fragrant steam billowed out. She placed the towel and robe inside and went back down the staircase. Sophia gestured with her elegant fingers splayed towards the bathroom.

"For you, Dana... enjoy," she said, and continued down the corridor.

I stepped into the warmth of the water and sighed. The bath was huge, and I thanked God for this Roman obsession. I slid so that the water sat just below my chin and felt that my body was cocooned in its warmth. In front of me, a panoramic window, remarkably unsteamed, looked out over Lake Alberto and the forest where I had walked only an hour or so before.

I thought of the vision of the woman, of the marble and the

images that came to me in the glade, and of Sophia's tea-leaf reading. I laid my head back in the water and felt the weight of my hair. I thought of my mother kneeling beside the bath, scooping water in a plastic jug and pouring it over my young head. I loved to look up into her face. She would round her lips to sing an accompaniment to the stream of water that broke in a crescendo on my head and back.

I closed my eyes and heard the drumming of my own heart. Again, I saw a procession of people and they were walking in time to that beat. This time they were not coming to me, but I was one of them, moving toward a woman, my woman, and she was reaching out across the spring toward me.

Madeleine returned alone. I was sitting in the salon by the fire, toasting my toes and flipping through magazines that seemed to feature Carlo in 10 years of varying hairstyles. Always there were women by his side. I was scrutinising one of these when she came in. I closed it immediately.

"Are you all right?" I asked. She had lost her shine.

"Yes." She discarded her bag on the floor and flopped on to the settee.

"You look relaxed, Dee. Where's Sophia?"

"Upstairs, I think. Where's Carlo?"

She shrugged her shoulders.

"Mads?"

"He's probably still going round in circles."

We smiled. At that moment Sophia came into the room. Madeleine jumped up.

"Madeleina?" Sophia moved towards her but looked back over her shoulder towards the front doors, "Carlo?" Her eyebrows puckered and I saw the resemblance between mother and son.

"Oh yes!" Madeleine forced the spirit back into her voice. "I was just worried about Dana."

The older woman relaxed. "Sì... naturale. As you see, your sister is... bene." She turned to leave, "I will ask Mariana to prepare for early supper."

Madeleine turned to me with a look of despair.

Thanking Sophia, I stood up and explained that we had to return to our hotel.

There was a pause like a breath held between us all. Madeleine's tension felt like a match ready to strike.

Sophia gave a small, sad nod. "Sì... I understand," she said quietly and stepped aside for us to leave.

Upstairs, I was bursting to know what had happened, but Madeleine was reluctant to talk. Between her clipped and half-hearted answers, I deduced her day. Carlo's minders had deposited her in a corporate box on her own, and he had not come near her for the entire day. She could see him, she said, if she followed the flash of cameras.

"I doubt he even knows I've gone," she said, zipping up the life bag. "Dee... am I a fool?"

"No!" I said, stifling a laugh, "You're not. He is!"

"Thanks," she said, without a hint of humour.

Sophia and Gaetano were waiting for us by the car. Sophia was reserved, and I wondered if she was all too familiar with her son's capricious relationships. She must have seen so many women – girls – come, and then go, yet she seemed genuinely sad. She kissed each of us on both cheeks and whispered in Madeleine's ear, which seemed to startle my sister for a moment. To me, she stroked my cheek then moved her hand to my chest.

"Dana... here... she waits for you."

I trembled. As we turned towards the car, neither Madeleine nor I could speak.

CHAPTER TWENTY-ONE

"Signorina." The concierge called me to the desk. He turned from the pigeonholes behind him and held out an envelope. Immediately I recognised the calligraphy. The muscles in my legs felt as though they were melting. Madeleine was holding the elevator door. She looked from my face to the envelope.

"Another one!"

We rode the three floors in silence. Our room seemed indifferent to our return, though it had now taken on a clinical smell. We sat, side by side on the closer bed and Madeleine watched as my trembling fingers released the note.

"What sort of a note is that?" she whispered, "It looks like a child's written it."

The content of the letter was made up of symbols – straight and waving lines. Madeleine took it from me. "Whoever's writing these, you'd think they'd include a translation!" she muttered as she studied the postmark. "It's from here, from Rome," she announced. "What's the point of these notes if you can't understand them?" My sister's face was tight with fatigue.

"I don't know." My heart felt as though it had dropped into my stomach, "But why would somebody go to all this trouble?"

She didn't respond.

I folded the note into the envelope and placed it with the other two in my suitcase. I sat down beside my sister and drew her to me.

"Mads..."

She gave one great sob and turned her head into my shoulder. "Bastard," was the only word I could hear among her tears.

We treated ourselves to dinner at an expensive restaurant we'd eyed since we arrived in Rome. The candlelit tables, the finely cooked veal and truffles were a welcome change from harsh practical lighting and the usual pasta and pizza. We talked lightly about our trip so far, able to laugh now about the ferry trip to Kos.

I didn't mention Julian, or the woman I'd thought I'd seen in the forest that morning. Madeleine and I hadn't been so close for many years, and I felt guilty for holding back. But I was becoming concerned about my experiences and, for the moment, wanted to keep them to myself. I feared that I was losing my grip on reality. We didn't discuss Carlo, either, though I doubted that he could be shaken off so easily. Madeleine had left her mobile phone at the hotel, and I pictured his messages stacking their weight against her resolve.

After a last mouthful of tiramisu, she put down her fork and carefully wiped the corner of her mouth with her napkin. "I called Julian," she said.

I lowered the fork that was suspended with shock in mid-air.

"After you thought you saw him," she said more quickly. "I just wanted to know if he was here."

"You didn't tell him that, did you?" All my anxieties and doubts about what I thought I'd seen rose to the surface.

She shook her head, "I said I was just wondering how he was. After all, he was part of my life too, like a brother for 10 years."

"And was he... is he... here?"

"He didn't say so... but then again, when it came to it, I forgot to ask. He was concerned about you."

"Why?"

"He hadn't heard from you for a while and..." She studied her empty bowl.

"He knows we're travelling," I said. "Obviously, he didn't get my letter. Anyway, I didn't think I had to tell him my movements."

"I know that... he knows that." Madeleine said, looking up. "Nevertheless, he's concerned."

"He could call me if he's so worried."

She shook her head and looked grieved. "Dee, sometimes you can be..."

I waited. A waiter whisked away our empty plates.

"Prickly," she said, at last and sat back in the seat with a "finally said it" satisfaction.

I collected tiny breadcrumbs on the tablecloth with the pad of one finger and placed them with care on to my napkin. "Your word or his?"

Madeleine leaned forward and tilted her head so that I was forced to look at her. "He still loves you."

"In the end, that doesn't mean anything. He chose to go to London or here or wherever he is and... anyway, you rang him!"

The waiter returned with coffees we hadn't ordered.

"Prego, signorine," he said, cupping his hands in a soft plea.

"Grazie." I was truly grateful for the distraction.

"There were no stones in the last two," I said.

Madeleine looked puzzled.

"With the letters."

"That's right! What could that mean?"

"Perhaps 'whoever' forgot to put them in."

"We never did work out what the stone was about," Madeleine said. "Maybe 'whoever' thinks we're dim and decided not to waste his time."

"Or hers," I said, "but we did sort of come to Rome because of the stone... and... Carlo."

"Did we?" Madeleine had become serious. "I wish we'd never gone to his hotel. Talk about looking eager – and easy."

Despite my reservations about Carlo, I doubted that he thought my sister was easy. There were times when I saw how tenderly he treated her. In truth, other than his reputation, and Madeleine's version of her day at the track, he had been a gentleman. I reminded myself that Sophia was his mother. She was too lovely, too refined to be the mother of a womaniser.

"What happened to Carlo's father?"

"Died years ago, when Carlo was a boy. He was a count or something."

"That would explain the villa," I said. "You'd think he'd move out of home by now."

"That is his home. Sophia lives with him. I think his father lost a lot of money. I'm not sure – Carlo didn't really go into it."

Madeleine's eyes glazed.

"Do you love him, Mads?"

She shook her head, but I could see that her eyes were smarting. I couldn't think of another time that I'd seen her this way over a man. Here we were, two "jiltees". When I told her this, she laughed.

"At least yours loves you," she said, "and that makes your situation more ridiculous than mine."

"More ridiculous than watching yours go round and round in circles?"

"Touché!" Madeleine blinked away the tears that had formed. "Though I wonder if we're all doing that – just going around in circles."

Our waiter appeared looking pleased with us. "The coffee is good, No?"

When we returned to the hotel, Madeleine's phone was swelling with messages.

"What should I do?" She was interrupted by the digital bars of Born to be Wild."

I shrugged my shoulders and went into the bathroom as she took the call.

Sitting on the closed toilet seat I could hear the murmur of her occasional answer. Carlo, I assumed, was sending rapid-fire questions across the broadband. I could picture him pacing the room, in circles. He would have a slim black phone pinned to his belt and his free hands would be pushing the point. I looked through the gap in the door. Madeleine was leaning back against the bed head. Her eyes scanned the ceiling as she listened. When she spoke, she sat forward and delivered her line with assertion.

"No Carlo. I don't know what your women are used to, but..."

I pulled the door closed and turned on the bath taps.

When I came back into the room, with some of my tension released down the plughole, Madeleine was sitting on the bed with the phone in her hand.

"Well?" I said.

"He's an arrogant bastard."

"So not much has changed," I said, though I could already hear the "but" in her voice.

"Dee."

Here it comes.

"He wants to make it up to me... tomorrow."

"Of course, he does," I said to the ceiling.

"Dee... Are you OK with this?"

"I just hope you know what you're doing."

"What will you do tomorrow?" she said, ignoring my comment.

"I'll think of something... I'm getting used to that."

"Ouch!" she said, with a teasing smile.

———

When Madeleine returned to the hotel after breakfast to prepare for her day out, I lingered over my coffee. I took out the mysterious notes from my bag and laid them side by side on the table.

That was three now – one delivered from Kos to me in Melbourne and written in Ancient Greek: "'Truth,' she said." And that was accompanied by a tiny marble stone that came not from Greece, but from the Apennines, including Italy. Then one delivered to me in Kos, written in Latin: "What you seek from me, you might have looked for nearer home," and in Rome, another, not written but delivered to my hotel with its symbols – straight and wavy lines, origins of the message unknown. The parchment-style paper of the three was the same, though the fibres and grains gave each its own character. Although it could have been recycled stationery, the quality seemed finer, more expensive.

I studied the words and symbols of each message that were exactly centred on each of the notes. The same hand had written at least the first two, evident in the tiny serif that occurred every now and then. At the end of the latest message was a small smudge that looked as if it had been hurriedly blotted. I had my first connection to its author.

What was someone trying to tell me? Who knew where to find me in Rome and where to find me in Greece? Could it be someone who had written an earlier hate letter?

The possibility frightened me, but those hate letters had been far from cryptic and had told me very clearly what their authors had meant. All but one of those had been typed, in bold. The one that had been handwritten had read: "Hope you die." It was crudely written, and the page had been torn roughly from a notepad so that its top edge was uneven. Though I couldn't be certain, I doubted these three were penned by that hand.

I picked up the first of the notes. At the time I'd received it, the court case was over and its arrival with the Kos postmark had propelled me on this journey. I placed it with the others and studied them all, looking for clues. I'd assumed the author to be male, though as far as I was aware none of the women I knew had been to Kos. I thought then of the woman in the Pantheon, but I had only seen her since I'd come to Rome. In the hard-surfaced reality of the café, I doubted her existence and scolded myself for giving my "visions" any credibility.

On the other hand, I wondered why I would invent her. Her face was as real as any individual around me now. I folded the notes and carefully placed them in my bag. Nothing was any clearer to me. I paid the bill and left.

CHAPTER TWENTY-TWO

The foyer of the city's library was expansive like an inflated lung and tracheated corridors led off it in several directions. A sign above each indicated subject areas and catalogue codes. I sat at one of the computers lining the wall that was still connected to the internet from the previous user.

I typed, "Giorni, Carlo," and looked guiltily over my shoulder as it loaded. Two hundred and seventy-three listings and Carlo featured in all those on the first page. I scrolled through the articles that lauded his skills on the track, his playboy antics and his injury. On the second page, in shorter and not so newsworthy articles, I found a rare photo of a humbler Carlo sitting with a child on her hospital bed. Anything for a photo opportunity, I thought. Further on I found what I wanted – the biography. I clicked the English translation.

'Carlo Giorni, premier Formula 1 driver for the fourth consecutive year, is not unused to the high life for which he is famous. Born in Florence in 1971, he is the only child of industrialist Caspare Giorni and Sophia Dubrova, the daughter of a

Romanian count. Educated at the Sorbonne, Carlo studied Philosophy and Law but abandoned his studies for the thrills of the racetrack, a decision that caused a rift between father and son. Caspare Giorni died in 1995 in a light-plane accident. He did not see the great heights to which his son climbed in Formula 1. The two did not reconcile...' The remainder of the article elaborated Carlo's success, but I felt that I was gaining some insight into the man who was supposedly entranced by my sister. I didn't trust him and was sure there was more to his story.

As I picked my way through the streets, I thought of Julian, but no longer looked for him in Rome. Madeleine's contact with him had rattled me. He still loves you, Madeleine had said but Julian would say that. He knew I'd been going through a difficult time since Bonnie's death and offered his distant, detached love as a support. My sister was a romantic and had never believed that Julian and I could break up. I wondered what this would mean for her today. Carlo was a smooth talker.

At the Pantheon, the guard nodded in recognition as I stepped through the doorway. I was convinced that my mind was playing tricks, perhaps a delayed response to the trauma of the past few months.

It was not a breakdown, I told myself and I was determined to find a logical explanation for the woman I had seen. There was little light inside, but I counted 30 others milling around the walls. One man stood in the centre looking up at the oculus aperture as the woman had done the first time I saw her and I studied the way the weak light reflected off his face, looking for any distortions to his appearance. I turned at the soft click of the side door. When I counted again, no one had come in, but someone had left.

The Minerva Piazza was less crowded than last time. I looked across to the steps of the church where I had seen the woman only days before. An elderly couple was descending each step as though it might crumble beneath their feet. I crossed the piazza and took those stairs two at a time. Inside, candles flickered in their holders on the walls. The church was crowded with tourists whispering in wonder at the stained glass, the architecture, and worshippers with eyes tight shut to block them out. One man with a shock of white hair sat in a back pew, his head bent back in a beseeching prayer. A middle-aged couple was admiring the workmanship of one of the Stations of the Cross on the far wall.

I took in the station closest to me, beautifully carved and gilded – *Jesus Falls the Third Time*. I followed the stations working backwards towards the main altar, stopping to consider each scene. *Jesus Falls the Second Time... the First Time.* I wished that life could be so easily rewound. Around him, his family and friends looked on with anguish, their paralysis caught with so much compassion in the wood of the carving. I recognised some of their expressions in the faces of those who had supported me during my own trial. What would I tell this Jesus of my adoring youth? Flee the garden? Go back to carpentry? Forget about saving people. What are you thinking? I mentally said to the fallen figure. His face was passive, shock had set in, and the crown of thorns pierced his head.

There were women in the background, and I knew which one was Mary – I'd seen that look on the face of mothers who watched their babies battle death. The other Mary was there, not so noble but stricken with grief. This face I loved, and so had the sculptor. This Mary's tears had formed tributaries around her eyes and mouth. There were other women there, behind the man, always veiled.

When I looked at that tableau, I felt that I was seeing it for the first time. Had I always focussed on the man and never the women behind? Had I done this in my own profession? I had always considered myself lucky to have no barriers to education and to my chosen field, but now, distanced from my work, I realised that perhaps I had been toeing the line. I had been taught, largely by men, about women's bodies and the process of birth, and it sat discordantly with me now.

Sightseers were spread through the recessed chapels and a line was filing past a structure at the main altar. When a gap appeared, I could see the sculpture of Catherine of Siena lying to face the vaulted heavens; beneath, her sarcophagus retained her headless body. I joined the crowd but gave up on jostling for a better look and chose instead to follow a passageway that led to a reconstruction of the rooms where she had lived. At a sharp right angle was a smaller corridor with a sign that simply read "Minerva".

Abandoning the reconstructed rooms, I followed the narrow steps that led into the foundations of the church. The staircase was lit with electric candles set into the wall but several of the globes had blown. There was no rail to guide me, and my left hand snatched at the wall for support. Halfway down, a young Nordic couple strode the steps confidently towards me but gave no acknowledgment of my presence other than to squeeze past me in single file.

Light from the chamber below had the density of a soft cumulus cloud that drifted on to the lowest steps to show their age and wear. Loose stones lay at the base of the staircase as if they had been washed there by a tide and I was reminded of the entropy of all things. The chamber was lit by massive candles in brass holders positioned to illuminate a slab of stone. The effect was magical, and I felt that I was in a scene from a Zeffirelli movie.

Several people were moving around the slab, pausing every now and then to read the plaques at its front. When I joined them, I allowed my fingers to caress its age-smoothed surface as

I had done at the altar to Asklepios. As the others left in a wave towards the steps, I glanced over my shoulder to the shadowed recesses and the doorway and, certain that I was alone for the moment, placed both palms firmly on the slab. The candles spluttered then righted themselves.

I closed my eyes and felt the stone drawing energy from my hands and pictured its molecules vibrating and expanding as it sucked at my core. I wondered how much I could lose when I felt a sensation of heat being returned to me, moving up my arms and into my body. My lids were closed as if paralysed and it was dark behind them as if the candles in the chamber had been extinguished.

Slowly the chamber became visible to me again and I looked down at the stone; its substance had dissolved, and I was staring into a great subterranean well. The candlelight behind me lit spot fires on the crest of tiny waves. Clouds of steam rose like smoke. I reached out and let my fingers drag in the gentle current. The water was warm and formed phosphorescent bubbles around each finger. Sulphurous air penetrated my lungs until I felt giddy, but I drank more of it.

I stepped into the healing spring and lowered my body, its structure separating first at my feet then up through each leg and into my arms, abdomen and chest. I lay my head back as I had in the hot springs of Kos and in Sophia's bath and felt the separation in my head. Only the tip of my nose lay above the water line connected to life-giving breath. Beneath the surface of the water, I could hear and feel a sonic pulse that accelerated my molecules at frenetic speed. Chaotic images in my mind fled as their vibrations increased. Gaps of light grew larger as the images dissipated. In those pure spaces an image was taking shape – a woman's face forming from folded light. Her lips, now complete, opened slowly to release a word ...

"Are you OK?"

A hand on my spine was dragging me through a dark tunnel. The rushed intake of air caught at the back of my throat, and I spluttered into the glow of the chamber. My hands were still fixed to the slab as another's hand slid from my back to my waist and a woman's face appeared at my shoulder.

"Steady," she said.

I breathed deeply.

"OK?"

"Yes... yes... thanks." I stood up straighter than I felt.

She was facing me now. "Do you need to sit? Should I call for help?"

I vaguely noted her New Zealand accent. I reassured her that I was all right, that I was giddy from not eating breakfast, and thanked her for her concern. In the awkward silence that followed, she left me, but not without a concerned look back over her shoulder as she went up the stairs.

Despite my smile of reassurance, my legs were weak and almost buckled beneath me when she disappeared. I was becoming very concerned now about these strange experiences that were becoming more frequent and more intense.

The very physical nature of this one had frightened me.

CHAPTER TWENTY-THREE

On the way back to the hotel, I had to stop several times to steady myself against light-headedness and a sense of disassociation of mind and limbs.

Could *I have a brain tumour?* It could account for some of my experiences. Fear constricted my throat as I pictured its steady growth in my brain. *Had it started its damage six months earlier?*

Was that why I found it so difficult to recall the exact events of Bonnie's death?

My legs refused to walk, and I leaned against the cool stone of an office building. Breath laboured against my paralysed diaphragm. I was certain that I must be pale; that I was about to collapse. No one stopped, though a middle-aged man paused briefly to give a nod of greeting. I looked beyond him to the opposite side of the road. A solitary figure was watching me, and I thought it was Julian, but I was desperate for proof now. I used the wall to propel me forward, but a bus passed between us. When it had gone, so had he.

At the hotel, I called his mobile phone, but the detached and slightly formal tone of his recorded voice stole my courage, and I left an awkward message, then regretted it.

I lay on the bed and read the hotel's brochures to distract my thoughts. The rattle of the door handle startled me. Madeleine made a small pirouette in the doorway as she extracted her key from the lock. I looked at my watch. "You're early."

"Hmmm?" She wore a look of Buddhistic calm.

"You're back sooner than I expected," I said, more curtly this time.

"Well, you know... I gave him a couple of hours. That will do... for now."

I wondered if my sister was speaking to me or to the ceiling.

"Obviously, you're happy enough with his explanation?" I was still lying down, and my own prone position seemed to heighten her dynamism.

"Oh yes..."

I saw her blush, but she continued: "He explained about the other day... I suppose I should just get used to his fame. In Italy, at least."

There was a small quiver in my chest, and I waited for her to continue, but she slid into the bathroom and closed the door softly. When she reappeared, the toilet seemed to be flushing more loudly than usual.

"How was your day, Dee?"

"OK..." I waited.

"What did you do?" This time, for the first time since Madeleine had come in, she looked me in the eye.

I held her gaze. "Not a lot."

She sat on the bed and leaned back on her arms to face me. Her sandalled feet were pointed into the carpet and her body formed a beautiful gradient against my base line. She looked at me with a serious expression. "I'm in love."

I sat up against the bed head and spoke to the architrave. "Is he?"

"He says he is."

"Can you believe him?"

Madeleine was studying my profile. "I think so."

I should have been happy for her, but I felt a foreboding sense of loss and knew I would regret wasting this moment of intimacy between us.

"That's great, Mads." I turned to her more fully now, trying to lift the level of enthusiasm in my voice, "What now?"

She took my hand. "For the moment, we'll have dinner and get on with our holiday."

Before eating, we took a long walk, diverting into unexplored lanes. Neither of us was a keen shopper, preferring to look through windows, but at one leather boutique, I fell in love.

"It's beautiful, Dee. You look stunning."

My reflection smiled in appreciation of the richness of the leather jacket. In the late afternoon light, the dark cobalt reflected in my eyes, and for a moment, I thought that I did look beautiful.

"Let me buy it for you."

Behind me, Madeleine sat in a deep, elegant armchair and together in the mirror we formed an old-fashioned daguerreotype, stained as if an inkwell had spilt across my chest. I imagined that photograph being passed between the fingers of Madeleine's children in time to come. They would see me smiling but ask why I was so sad. I looked at my face and the eyes that reflected the dusty Roman light and I realised that I had become a victim of my own life.

Madeleine's phone jarred me into real time. She fumbled in her bag, embarrassed by the ringtone, though the shop assistant had moved on to another customer.

"Dad? Is everything all right?"

I turned from the mirror as I took off the coat. She was listening intently but smiled at me with reassurance.

"Ah ha..." The phone was cradled under one ear while she extracted a credit card from her wallet.

The conversation was brief, and it occurred to me that she and my parents had been in regular contact.

"Dad's been trying to call you. Ruth has rung to let you know there's a conference in England you might be interested in." She took the coat from me.

"Didn't Dad want to talk to me?"

She shrugged. "I think they know that you want to be left alone." She was still admiring the coat as she took it to the counter. "How great's this jacket?"

I turned back to the mirror. I was devoid of colour.

As we stepped out into the street, Madeleine gave me the laminated carry bag. Inside, my new jacket was cushioned luxuriously in a wad of white tissue paper. The colour contrast reminded me of Kos and how far we had come, physically at least.

"Mads, this is such an expensive gift..."

Her face had a look of warning.

"Thanks so much. It's... the best present I've ever had."

She smiled. "And so is this holiday!"

We walked on.

"Did Dad tell you what the conference is about?"

"No. Are you interested?" She had paused and was facing me with a look of anticipation.

I kept my pace.

"Dee?"

I stopped. I had to admit to feeling a little excited at the thought of a conference.

"I'll call Ruth," I said, to satisfy my sister.

She didn't reply, but when we continued our walk, I noted her small smile.

The pot of Earl Grey tea, a rare find in Rome, steamed between us.

"So, will you call Ruth?" Madeleine was stirring her sugarless cup.

I shrugged my shoulders as I tried to fathom the bottom of mine.

"Go on," she urged, nodding in the direction of my bag that was strung across the back of the chair.

Obediently, I took out the phone and switched it on. Three new voice messages rumbled inside. The first was from Ruth. The sound of her voice distressed me initially; it was a voice that could compel people to reveal their most personal secrets. I missed her. The conference was in Bath the following week, though she didn't have many details. As she recited the contact number, I was reminded of the weekly staff meetings that she would chair. In my mind, I took in my colleagues – mostly men. Did they ever think it odd that they predominated in obstetrics? These were good men. I knew each of them very well. Most of them were highly regarded and I would have had no qualms about any of them delivering my own child, but now I longed for the company of women. I wanted to belong to that band of women surrounding the fallen Christ – Mary of the womb, Mary at the tomb.

"God bless, Dana," Ruth whispered through the diodes of my phone. I clicked off.

Madeleine watched me. I relayed the message and she waited for me to continue.

"She's left the number, if I'm interested."

"It would be good for you," she said, seeming satisfied.

"And for you?"

She looked hurt. "What do you mean?"

I told her what I meant.

"Dee... you are the most important person in my life. This holiday has been something I've wanted for so long. Now that I finally have my sister back, I don't want this to end."

"Where am I back from?"

That dewy look was condensing in my sister's eyes. She leaned towards me across the table.

"Do you remember when we were kids, we spent so much time together playing? We didn't really need anyone else. Even when you were a teenager, you still had time for me, though I must have been dragging at your heels."

I smiled to myself at the strange role-reversal now.

She went on, "But when you went to uni, we drifted apart..."

"But that's normal, surely?" I was feeling defensive.

"Of course. But it's not that. You changed. You were always so easy-going, calm... spiritual, even. Everybody noticed that about you. I admired you so much and I still do."

I breathed deeply to muster a defence but accepted there was some truth in it. Though I couldn't pinpoint where or why, I acknowledged that I had become more reserved, perhaps I had become brittle. My voice came out in a plaintive whisper: "Do you still admire me?"

My sister sat back. Her smile was radiant, "More than anyone else. You are so clever, so beautiful. I'm in awe of you."

"But I've failed."

She raised her eyebrows in frustration. "It wasn't your fault! You've dealt with death before and it had to come – being blamed." She raised her cup for a toast: "Onward and upward."

"Amen to that," I said, and placed my hand on the rich leather of my new coat.

CHAPTER TWENTY-FOUR

A jolt of conscience woke me in the middle of the night. I sat up and switched on the lamp. Madeleine was softly snoring.

The digital voice of the phone's inbox rambled through its spiel.

"Message one. Left at…"

"Hello, darling, it's Dad…" I clicked off sending a mental apology to my father.

"Message two. Left at…"

"Dana…" The sudden rise of blood pressure in my head distorted Julian's next words. I sat upright, taming slept-on hair with my free hand.

"Got your message – well, at least your hello. Are you all right? Call me again."

That was all. I hit replay listening for something else, a clue to the emotion in his voice. I tried to recall the tone I might have heard him use when talking to a friend on the phone, or was it the way he sounded in more intimate moments with me? I wanted to envisage him sitting alone in his office and wondered if he had set it up like his room in the home we'd shared.

Did he still have the photograph of me that he had loved, the one where he caught me spinning like a child outside the tent we had finally managed to erect? Emotion gripped my chest as I thought of that holiday. We'd never felt so free. We'd never been so in love. The image was fractured by one tiny sound in the background. I replayed it again. It was the faint clink of crockery, the pitch that just two dinner plates might make in an intimate room as they were being cleared from the table.

My head groaned against the bed head.

Madeleine stirred and looked at me with one open eye. "What's up?" she mumbled through the sheet that covered her mouth. She sat up. "Dee?"

Though I felt foolish, I told her what I had heard.

"Give me the phone." She held out her hand in a command. "Let me hear it."

I shook my head. "I've deleted it."

"He called you, right?" There was a look of undisguised exasperation on my sister's face. "That says something!"

"The little notes say something, but we don't know what they mean, either." I wondered which was more difficult to decipher, cryptic letters or human nature.

While Madeleine was showering the next morning, I called the phone number Ruth had left for the conference in Bath. It would begin in two days, I was told by a very serious male voice. I pictured him wearing a shirt with a top button that strained at his throat. His hair would be black, greased so that it looked like a helmet. He would be standing, the phone held just away from the ear.

"At this late notice," he said, "you would need to find your own accommodation. Would you like to register?"

There was a pause and I wondered if he was hoping I would say no.

I hesitated. "Yes."

As I gave my details and my medical title, I felt an odd tug as if between an old and a new self. When I turned off the phone, I all but threw it on the bed as if it had been complicit in a crime.

Steam puffed from the bathroom. Madeleine came out, rubbing her hair with a towel, her rosy-brown flesh vibrant with health. She stopped when she saw me staring at the phone.

"Are you going?"

"Yes."

She smiled and resumed rubbing her head.

"Are you sure you won't come?" I asked.

"It's important that you go. I'll come if you want me to, but..."

I raised my hand to stop her. Yes, she would come if I wanted her to, but she was right. I needed to go on my own, and I needed to give her space, and more time with Carlo.

"It's OK," I said. "I'll just be a couple of days, and it would be boring for you."

She stepped into her jeans and jumper. "Bath sounds nice... but..."

You're a Roman now, I wanted to say.

I spent the rest of the morning booking a flight for the following day and organising accommodation. Despite the receptionist's misgivings, it was relatively easy to find a room near the university where the conference was to be held. I made a mental note to tell him.

It had been many years since I'd been to England, though I'd never visited Bath. My impression had been that it was too staid and conservative for my tastes, though Madeleine would probably have thought that it would suit me well. I had stayed with friends in London for a month during my student years. I'd like to think that I'd painted the town red, but, in truth, I'd spent most of the time swotting in the Oxford Medical Library. I went to the predictable sites, saw 'The Mousetrap' and drank a few warm pints of Guinness. I remembered Madeleine's bewildered look when I came home and told her about my time away. She left for Europe not long after. Her holiday was a total antithesis of my own, as if to make a point. I remembered, too, that she had asked me to go with her, but I was bored with travel and keen to get back to my thesis. For a moment, I strained to remember what my thesis had been about, and it occurred to me that, in the long run, it hadn't really mattered. I should have gone with my sister; there would have been a lot to remember.

———

Madeleine was out with Carlo. I could picture his smile of satisfaction knowing I was out of the way, for a few days at least. My sister tried to disguise her buoyancy with long *I'll miss you* hugs and did offer to spend the day with me.

"No," I said firmly, releasing her from her sisterly duty and myself from her grip. In the street, I saw how a passer-by moved aside as the two of them gushed through the hotel's entrance and on to the pavement; how Madeleine almost leapt into the passenger seat of Carlo's black convertible and how, as he planted his foot to the accelerator, the traffic seemed to pause to accommodate him as if he controlled the elements. This was a man who had to be ahead. I hoped not at any cost.

It didn't take long to pack. I'd been living in much the same clothes – jeans and T-shirt – for weeks. For a conference, though, I would need something dressy and felt pleasure at the thought that it might be the perfect chance to debut my new blue leather jacket. I did a mental stocktake of the clothes in my bag and decided that I had to go shopping. A day spent shopping among Roman fashion boutiques would distract me from returning to the Pantheon.

Though I was in a crowded and bustling city, it seemed that each day as I walked I saw familiar faces: the old woman with the terrier, both stiff-hipped and wearing matching red tartan coats; the white-haired man who stood at the door of his apartment and watched the world go by at any time of the day; the young nanny with her three charges, two boys and a baby in the pram whom she handled with the love and ease of a parent.

Four hours later, I returned. I had managed to overlook the stylish and expensive designs to find, with considerable effort, simple black pants and a jumper, truly a Melbourne girl. But I surprised myself with the thrill I had in buying stationery for the conference – the leather-bound journal nestling in the tissues of its box, and an overly ornate pen. An iPad would not have cost that much more, I reasoned, but I felt great satisfaction as the pen slid easily from its sheath and I swept my hand as though writing invisible calligraphy in the air.

Madeleine returned looking furtive, but content. She didn't give away much about her day and, when I asked, she steered the conversation back to mine. But even as I related my shopping trip, and showed her the purchases, she seemed to be forcing herself to concentrate. She overcompensated with repeated exclamations of: "Great!"

"Are you excited?" she said.

"About going to a conference? Not particularly."

"I bought you something today."

I hadn't noticed the brown shopping bag in her hand until she extended it towards me.

"Mads... you shouldn't have! You've already bought me enough!" I glanced across at my jacket hanging on the cupboard door.

"Just something small," she said, shaking the bag at me with insistence.

Inside was a fine cashmere scarf in brown and the cobalt blue of the coat.

"It's beautiful!" I wrapped it loosely around my neck. The feeling was sensual as it ran through my fingers. I slid the jacket from its hanger, put it on and turned towards Madeleine. She was smiling broadly as she tweaked at the collar of the coat and adjusted the scarf. This time, I felt like her daughter dressing for a date.

"Perfect," she said, "you could wear it tonight."

Across my hesitation, she continued, "Carlo wants to take us out for dinner before you go."

"And whatever Carlo wants..." I protested. I wanted a quiet night.

"Oh, come on, Dee!" Madeleine was bursting with a mix of enthusiasm and irritation. "London's not that far away."

"Exactly! So why the farewell dinner?"

She looked upset and I regretted my tone.

"He's made the reservation," she said, with some finality.

I took off the scarf, hung up the jacket and prepared to shower.

CHAPTER TWENTY-FIVE

The restaurant was close to our hotel and one we both recognised. We had walked past it several times and, in the evenings, the candlelit tables and quiet opulence of the red and black furnishings had been intimidating to two single sisters.

The maître d' ushered us to a table set for three in the centre of the room. I'd noticed my sister's blush of embarrassed pleasure at the immediate attention Carlo's name prompted. As she walked ahead of me, I sensed that it could be easy for her to slip into the pseudo-royalty of Italy's jet-set.

At the table, we sat in self-conscious silence as we waited for our host. While Madeleine pondered the menu with too much interest, I took in the other patrons, mostly couples. Some seemed to be in the animated and slightly awkward conversation of a new relationship. I watched as an older couple exchanged a few words loaded with decades of mutual understanding. Her fingers, heavy with diamonds, paused above the plate – knife and fork caught in mid-air. She smiled at him in acknowledgement of something he murmured to her across the rim of his wine glass. Before replying, she carefully placed the knife and fork on the plate and sipped her wine while he resumed his meal. Several times they worked this way, their conversation a beautiful dance of intimacy.

At a corner table an elderly woman sat facing the restaurant, my own preferred position. She appeared to be on her own, despite the setting opposite her. At one point, a waitress came to take it away and she waved her off. The woman had a commanding presence, but her eyes held a sorrow. I imagined that the setting was for a husband who was not returning.

When Julian and I had dined out, I would always choose the seat that faced the other patrons and wondered that he never complained about always facing the wall behind me. I mentioned it once, offering to change places, but he said he didn't need to look at anyone else in the room.

I broke off a portion of bread to satisfy the gnawing in my stomach. After 10 minutes or more Carlo entered, and the maître d' greeted him affectionately. He was dressed in a flaming red shirt and slim black pants and stood to take in the restaurant as though he owned it. Many of the diners paused to watch him. Straight-backed and elegant, he carried with him an energy, heightened by the slight limp that discharged a spark at each table he passed. In the candlelit glow of my sister's eyes, I could see that she was his conduit.

"I am the luckiest man in the room," he said, as he approached us. He kissed Madeleine on both cheeks, lingering by her ear in an intimacy that made me breathless.

"Bella, Dana," he said, eyeing my scarf and jacket that I had elected to keep on.

I acknowledged the flattery wordlessly. Madeleine might be charged by this man's energy, but he drained my own.

When he was seated, a waiter poured his wine. I watched as he lifted the glass to his lips, cupping the stem between his second and third fingers, the ring from my dreams angled towards me in a taunt. The dipping and rising of his hand mesmerised me and my peripheral vision became blurred like a memory scene in a TV soap opera.

The ring's gold pattern of oak leaves was set against a deep blue background, the colour of the Aegean. Across the enamelled sea, a tiny boat manouevred between golden peninsulas. I focussed closer. The boat was larger than I had first thought and had a deep wooden hull. Within it, semi-naked men rowed to a hypnotic chant that swung between stern and bow like a pendulum. Between their feet, glistening with sprays of sweat and sea water lay an immense brown snake. The men seemed unconcerned by its presence but rowed with a determination driven by their serpentine companion. I zoomed in closer, following the line of the tapering tail back to the head which rested on the bow with the serenity of a sage. As it breathed, each coppery scale detached from the next then contracted back again, and it was this rhythm of breath that set the rowers' pace. It turned its massive head as though aware of my presence, though acknowledgement came only as a small dilation and constriction of an eye's lens, so dark and deep it was like a passage to the underworld. It turned its head back to sea in a gesture that willed me to follow. Ahead, the golden oak leaves of land called the boat forward.

"Dee..."

My sister's voice called from behind me. I didn't acknowledge immediately but stayed transfixed on the journey ahead until the land, sea and the boat dissolved. A glass of sparkling wine from Chianti had been placed before me. Madeleine and Carlo were waiting expectantly, and I thought of the boat being washed by the bubbling spray of a menacing wave.

"I'm only going to Bath," I said, clinking my glass with

theirs and realising that this might well be cause for their cele-bration.

"There is another reason, Dee." Between the candlelight and the effervescence of her wine, Madeleine's furrowed eyebrows couldn't hide her radiance. I glanced again at the ring on Carlo's hand. The boat waited, and the oarsmen readied for the swell building beneath them.

"There is?" I said, still not facing her.

She reached forward and touched the back of my hand, "Carlo has asked me to marry him."

I felt the slack of her fingers as I failed to reply. When I finally met their eyes, Carlo was watching me with a look of derision. My sister's face had relaxed into a form of detach-ment. I lifted my glass that now felt heavier than before.

"Congratulations."

I hated myself for my meanness, and I forced enthusiasm into my voice as I asked for the details. Madeleine enthusiastically recounted Carlo's proposal, pausing only to place her order with the waiter. It was as clichéd as I would have predicted – lunch in another exclusive restaurant, but with enough patrons to applaud the bent knee.

"No ring?"

"He wants to choose it with me in Paris," she explained. But I wondered.

"And you did... say yes?"

"I'll be back from Paris before you are," she said, and added hurriedly "We can... go somewhere..." Her forehead creased. She knew it was not going to be the same now.

"Dana." Again, that voice greased the space between us.

"You are happy for your sister, no?" One eyebrow was propped with sarcasm.

"My sister's happiness is very important to me, Carlo. I hope that it is for you, too."

Madeleine inhaled and let out a sigh that carried my name forward in a headwind.

I continued, framing impertinent questions with false politeness. I cross-examined him about his life – the little I knew and what I had read, and he answered me each time with some amusement. My sister fidgeted with the corner of her napkin and gazed distractedly around the restaurant. When the meal was set down, she seemed grateful for the interruption and made too much fuss of simple fare.

"Your father died. Madeleine has told me. What happened?"

There was a small flicker of something – rage or sorrow, but I wasn't ashamed. He hesitated and his aquiline nose flared at the nostrils as he took his breath. He spread his hands on the table.

"A light-plane accident, Dana... the cause was never determined."

"And Sophia?" I continued. "It must have been a great shock."

Did the hands twitch?

"Sì, a shock." He looked at me gravely. "But, for Sophia, was not great sorrow." He saw my reaction and continued: "My father was... tyranny."

There was an uncomfortable pause and Madeleine was watching me with bewilderment.

I persevered. "I believe he was a Count?"

"I told Dana about your father, Carlo," Madeleine said, giving me a "look" out the corner of her eye.

When he turned to my sister his face softened. "Sì, Dana,"

he said, turning back and clasping Madeleine's nearest hand on the table. The move was soft, and his thumb stroked her skin. "In Italia," he said, "these traditions and titles should be... obsolete. My father's wealth came not from title, but from his business – marble. All Italia is made of marble!" He laughed before becoming serious again. "My mother, she is true Countess." He touched his free fist to his heart. "She did not know my father's dealings. Sophia always assumes best... the most decency. Over time she understands her husband is not so decent."

"She didn't leave?" I asked.

Carlo touched his heart again. "My mother is proud... and has strong belief in God. Divorce is not possible."

"Are you religious, Carlo?"

Madeleine's eyes fluttered as I asked the question, whether from irritation or not, I couldn't tell.

"Sì... of course. I am Italian!" He said it glibly, but his free hand moved to his throat and removed a gold chain and locket from under his shirt. Inside the locket was a Byzantine image of the Madonna, beautiful in its simplicity. The opposite face was empty. "This place," he said, running his finger inside, "is for Madeleina."

I sat back and observed their tender looks. There were moments when he was talking that I could see what my sister saw in him. But there was no photo of her in the locket, no ring on her finger. Was he his father's or his mother's son?

I thought of Sophia, and because of her, I maintained some hope. I couldn't deny that Madeleine was happy, and I needed to assume that Carlo truly loved her. When I resigned myself to it, I felt a sinking, draining sensation. I was jealous. In Carlo's presence, I was witnessing the transformation of my sister, though perhaps love had always done that, and I just had never seen the gilding of Madeleine.

Though she was always warm and humorous, tonight, as

the dinner progressed, she became more relaxed as though lit with an internal heat that gave her limbs a languid grace. She was not one of the modelesque beauties who usually surrounded the famous driver, but in that moment, I thought I saw her through his eyes. Madeleine's vibrancy and inner beauty shone. When Carlo raised a dark, black cherry to my sister's lips I looked away.

At another table, a couple paused to clink their glasses in celebration. From where I sat, light reflected from the woman's eyes and refracted through the champagne bubbles of her glass. The man smiled at something she said and his voice in reply was warm and rich. On the wall above their heads, a painted cornucopia spilled grapes and melons on to a tablecloth of golden silk.

As we sipped the last of our coffee, silence clung to the air between us.

"Mads," I said, "why don't you stay with Carlo tonight? I'm tired now and I've got an early flight."

She looked startled. "No way, Dee, I want to see you off!"

"I'd rather go on my own. The taxi's been organised," I lied.

Madeleine looked hurt. "Are you sure?"

"Yes," I said, picking up my handbag and half-standing.

The two of them rose with me.

"Dana, we will walk you home," Carlo said, already preparing to leave with me.

"No," I insisted, "it's a short block and it's still early. The streets are busy."

He was about to object but saw my own determination.

"Stay on," I said. "This is your engagement night!" I kissed Madeleine's cheek. "I'll call you from Bath when I get there, and I'll see you in a week. Enjoy Paris."

She looked anxious as she cupped my face and kissed my cheek. "Be careful."

At the door, I looked back at them. Madeleine and Carlo were seated, but had turned towards me, their hearts facing each other.

———

As I hung my jacket in the wardrobe, I turned and took in our hotel room. Though Madeleine's belongings were still there, it felt as if she had already left. Her bed retained the imprint of where she had sat, preserved like a ghostly reminder of my solitude. Although I didn't feel a great enthusiasm for the conference, I was glad now that I was going.

I checked my phone. No messages. I had wanted to escape all that I knew, and it now seemed that I had done just that.

———

The taxi I had ordered arrived promptly, and I had more time than I needed at Fiumicino Airport. While I waited for my flight, I drank too much coffee and browsed through endless magazine racks until, under the suspicious gaze of one proprietor, I felt the need at least to buy a newspaper. Again, political news dominated the front page, but, on page three, I was startled by a photograph of Madeleine and Carlo, arm in arm, leaving the restaurant from the night before. The caption read simply: "Amore... amore... amore..." Madeleine was becoming another page-three statistic.

The phone vibrated in my bag that was sandwiched between my feet. It was Madeleine. While she wished me bon voyage, I considered her happy profile in the paper before me.

"Have you seen today's newspaper?" I asked. In the brief silence before she answered, I sensed her blushing.

"Yes, Carlo showed me."

Typical, I thought, that he would scan the newspapers for evidence of his popularity. Was my sister just a new angle to keep up his profile?

"He was angry," she continued. "He wants us to be left alone."

"Perhaps, when you're married, he'll lose his appeal," I offered.

"For me, or the public?" Madeleine enquired, laughing.

I took too long to answer.

CHAPTER TWENTY-SIX

AVEBURY

As Rome diminished beneath the plane's wings, I felt a small sense of relief. It was the age, the beauty and the passion of that city that had affected me, I decided. My emotions had heightened, I reasoned, manifesting in fanciful visions of the woman. A medical conference would restore my rationality and I would see things more objectively, I assured myself.

I settled back into the seat, wondering what my sister was doing. Was she looking out at Sophia's garden and the herbs that she knew better by their botanical names? Would she glance towards the sky to look for me, or had Carlo fixed his position before her?

I closed my eyes and drifted into a soft daydream. Sophia's face met mine. She was smiling, though her warm, flecked eyes seemed to be appealing to me to do something, to see something. Was it to do with her son? As I studied her face it began a slow transformation, younger, fair-headed – the woman in the Pantheon. Her full lips puckered around a word that I strained to hear... Who? Soo? Before me she deconstructed into shards like a broken mirror that reflected my own face.

"Tea? Coffee?"

I coalesced into the seat. My mouth that had taken on the shape of the woman's exclamation had to reform around a reply.

The plane landed with a shudder that resonated to my core. Through the window, grey clouds that seemed to follow me from one country to another clustered into brooding, theatrical forms. Predictably, the check-out was painstakingly slow, but I was amazed and relieved to see my bag first out on to the carousel. In Rome, I had felt lonely while Madeleine was with Carlo, but now I relished having time to myself. I elected to take the slower coach rather than the train from Heathrow to Bath.

In the subterranean world beneath the station, I found the bay and a bus that was already taking passengers. There were few people on board as I settled into a seat by a window, leaving my handbag and jacket on the one next to me as a dissuasion. A procession of travellers began boarding and, reluctantly I removed them as an apologetic-looking man filled the space. I smiled and quickly turned my face to the window, the glass and the concrete wall outside forming a mirror that reflected my companion and me. He was angled away and he, too, seemed intent on a distraction through the opposite windows. I noted his clothing – mid-grey linen suit, white shirt. He was immaculately groomed. His profile, now forward-facing, was of a man in his early forties. He leaned his head back into the headrest and closed his eyes. I turned away from the window and glanced down at his hands that were resting, palm down, on his knees. Manicured fingers; no ring.

Where would he be going? Why would I wonder?

It was only when the coach launched itself into the gloomy daylight that he stirred. I resisted the urge to turn away.

"Another sunny English day," he said, in a Hugh Grant-style voice, to the rear of the seat in front of me as though he needed the light before he could speak.

I made a sound of amusement but couldn't think of anything to add. There was an awkward silence that I knew punctuated too many of my real or potential conversations. I had never been good at small talk. Madeleine, on the other hand, seemed to be able to find endless points of discussion, even with people she didn't know. Where once this might have irritated me, now I saw that it was an expression of her genuine interest in others, while mine could be seen as a position of arrogance and self-centredness.

"England – beautiful one day, perfect the next," I offered, but the moment had gone, and I realised, with acute embarrassment, that he would not be familiar with advertisements for sunny Queensland. It was greeted with bewildered amusement.

For several minutes, we continued in silence on our journey. Nothing improved outside. The sky, road and buildings all seemed to be variations of grey. Above the murmurs of the other passengers, music filtered through the speakers and formed a sombre soundtrack that seemed to heighten the strain between my fellow passenger and me as if something needed to be said. I wished I'd brought a book.

"Are you travelling far?" he said, turning to face me.

I angled towards him "To Bath."

He was a man with a handsome profile. Full faced, he was... interesting, that dreaded word that haunted people considered to be plain. But in his case, it was true. Certainly, his eyes were a feature. Thick, fair lashes only allowed glimpses of deep-blue eyes. Nordic came to mind. His face was deeply pock-marked and gave him a craggy appearance. I thought he was very attractive.

"And you?" I said, a little more self-conscious now.

"To Avebury."

"I don't know that area."

"You're Australian." He was speaking to my eyes but there was a sense of my whole face being taken in.

"Is it the accent?" I said, feigning naivety.

"It's charming." His gaze had moved to my lips.

I was riveted by those lashes – dark at the roots and long enough to be sun-kissed at the tip. When he looked up the move was languid, sensual. I couldn't look away.

"Are you from Avebury?"

"No," he said, looking away briefly, "I have business there. Other than its Georgian splendours, why are you visiting Bath?"

"Perhaps it's just for its Georgian splendours."

Again, his eyes tracked over my face as if making an assessment. "No, I don't think so. I also have an idea that you would dare not to be a fan of Jane Austen."

"She was a brilliant writer."

"Don't disappoint me."

I smiled at that. In truth, I wasn't a great fan. "There's a conference I'm interested in. Tell me about Avebury."

"If we're going to be that intimate then I think we should exchange names. I'm Elliot," he said, raising his hand towards me.

"Dana." I took it. His palm was warm, but I withdrew my own quickly.

"Avebury is... quaint," he said, derisively, returning his

hand to his knee, "but every now and then," he continued, "in such backwaters, a gem is uncovered. Avebury's beauty lies in its fields."

"And the gem?" I said, intrigued now.

Before he could answer the coach braked suddenly. Other passengers twittered when the coach driver yelled out the window as we lurched past the car in front.

"Dana," he said, once we were moving again, "tell me what's interesting about your conference."

I hesitated. Was I interested?

For the moment, I'd forgotten about it and wondered why I'd ever signed up. At that moment, I was content to chat to this stranger, and to soak up the meagre sun when the clouds parted. I realised that, since Bonnie's death, I had hardly ever been alone. Madeleine, especially, had always been there. The thought that I wasn't surrounded by family and well-meaning friends who watched me from the corner of their eyes was liberating. I turned to face my stranger fully.

"It's on the history of obstetrics."

Elliot's face twitched. I raised my eyebrows.

"I'm sorry, Dana. It sounds a bit... dry. What's to know? Women have always given birth. Are you an historian?"

I paused. "No, I'm an obstetrician." From the pit of my stomach something stirred. I could feel its energy run the length of my spine, into my scalp.

Elliot bowed his head slightly and I thought I detected a rise in the colour of his cheeks.

"I'm sorry. What a gaff. You must think me to be a real nob. It's just... you don't look like a..."

"Man?"

"You certainly don't look like a man," he said, lowering those beautiful lashes as, again, he studied the line of my lips.

I shuffled slightly in my seat.

"The conference then," he said, looking into my eyes.

I thought of how briefly I'd scanned the program. "I'll be there for the lectures on midwifery. There's a move to acknowledge the role of women in delivery."

"A token effort?" he said, showing more interest this time, "But why Bath? I could understand it being in Glastonbury. Or Avebury, for that matter."

"Are you associating midwifery with the occult?"

He paused and looked thoughtful. "I'm a dealer in antiquities, and I'm heading to Avebury hoping to purchase a votive offering that depicts a mother and child. It was found at the site of a Celtic dig."

I thought that they would have been common enough and said this to him.

"Yes," he said, "but this one is carved in marble. Most unusual here. All other votives found in this area have been carved from local limestone."

The bus lurched to a stop. The driver held his hand down on the horn. I waited for another verbal assault but saw only an overweight Labrador saunter to the kerb. The driver huffed through the gears.

Elliot explained that there had been little trade in the area at the time attributed to the dig where the votive had been found.

"The Romans?" I offered.

His smile was mildly patronising. "It predates the Romans."

When I asked him how he knew, he looked puzzled.

"We seem to be very good at insulting each other," he said. "Rather advanced for us, don't you think? That usually occurs much later." He was giving me that look again. I could feel the colour rising in my cheeks.

"Are you hot?" he said, with mock concern.

I blazed.

"It's very... appealing."

My bag was between my feet, and I bent down to it, feeling for the pocket and drew out the letters and stone.

"This may not be your area, but... can you tell me anything about this?" When I placed the stone in the palm of his hand, it looked so insignificant.

"I'm not a geologist," he said.

Disappointed, I went to take it back.

"Where did you get this?" He ignored my open palm.

Though I didn't understand why, I told him my story, about Bonnie, about the stone and the letters and perhaps because he was a stranger, it had a cathartic effect. As I spoke, he glanced from me to his palm that still cupped the stone, and back again as if constructing a skeleton on which to hang his image of me. Where Alexander had listened with serious interest, I found Elliot's face hard to read. To the ears of this Englishman, my story must have seemed fanciful. Though his expression gave nothing away, he studied the stone with a professional eye.

"There's an unusual pink streak..." he said, thoughtfully. "I should have liked to have seen a larger sample."

I told him about Alexander, and how he thought it might have come from the Apennines, but he didn't seem to be listening. He turned the stone over in his palm. Finally, he closed his fingers over it and gave it back to me, looking at the notes still sitting in my lap.

"An interesting story, Dana. Do you know who wrote the notes?" He put his hand out as though expecting to see them.

"That's a bigger mystery," I said, as I gave them to him.

"Sounds like an admirer."

I told him how I'd thought about every person I knew, but always drew a blank.

"The strangest thing is that whoever it is seems to know

where I am... and the later letters were posted locally. Then there's the obscurity of the words, and their connection to the stone, if any."

He had been reading the letters as I spoke, and they were still in his lap. "Perhaps you would be better visiting Glastonbury." I knew that Glastonbury was a magnet for hippies and New-Age culture. Annoyed, I took the notes from his knees.

There was a silence between us now. The overcast sky and I glared at each other through the window. The coach eased into a curb and an elderly couple seated at the front took their time to get off. They seemed to know the driver as there was a back and forth of conversation. Mentally I pushed them off the bus. I was annoyed with myself now that I'd made the effort at small talk. It never stayed small. When the coach took off again, Elliot was quiet, and I wondered if he thought the same.

"Again, I'm sorry, Dana," he said, close to my hair. I didn't turn to him. I was angry with his insinuation, but, at the same time I felt a rush of adrenalin and something dilating in my lower abdomen. I lay my head back into the headrest and took a deep breath.

"No problem," I said, closing my eyes to avoid looking at him.

"Could I see the stone again?"

When I looked at him, he was blushing. I took it out and gave it, reluctantly, to him.

"See this," he said, pointing to the pink vein in the marble, "I've seen this sort of marking before. It was a votive offering from Wessex. The piece I mention was very old, very rare... and sold for a great deal."

"And you were the dealer."

There was a twitch of pleasure around his mouth. "I was."

"Do you think it could be the same rock?"

"It would be damn exciting if it was, but it's too small, I'm afraid."

"So," I said, more to myself than to him, "I have one stone, three notes – one from Kos with Greek words attributed to Hippocrates, one from Rome in Latin, and the third?" I offered it to him.

"Yes," he said, taking it. "This is early Celtic; I can tell you that for certain – around 800 BCE is my guess. You'd think this would be the easiest of the three notes for me, but the language had so many dialects and, there isn't that much around. I do have someone in Glastonbury, though..."

He flinched under my glare but continued: "And I'll be seeing him this trip, as it happens."

"Because of the Avebury piece?"

He nodded. "Also marble, as I said. I'm hoping as old as the Wessex piece. There's an inscription on it, I believe, but apparently, it's so old and worn, it's barely decipherable. That's why I need him. He knows enough about the language to put together the most rudimentary clues." He paused and considered me, "Why don't you come with me... and bring your note?"

Before the refusal left my lips I hesitated. I was tempted by the possibility of solving at least part of the riddle. Elliot didn't wait long for an answer. "We could stay in Avebury tonight, and set out for Glastonbury in the morning."

"I'm on my way to Bath... for a conference," I said, rather feebly.

"Separate rooms, of course."

CHAPTER TWENTY-SEVEN

Though his gallant assurance was meant as an incentive, I reminded myself that I knew very little about this man. How could I simply get off the bus with him – separate rooms or not? I tried to imagine explaining myself to Madeleine, but all I could think of were the lovesick looks she and Carlo would be giving each other.

"OK," I said suddenly and surprising myself. "Separate rooms, and to Glastonbury tomorrow."

His mouth curled into a smile that I hoped was not a leer. "Great," he said, patting my knee and I wondered if I was making a mistake.

"Avebury's the next stop," he said, removing his hand and standing up to collect his bag from the overhead locker.

"By the way," I said, "why the bus, rather than driving?"

He looked down between his arms. "A little matter of drinking and driving."

"I see." My heart was pounding as I picked up my hand bag. I looked out the window hoping for some confirmation in the clouds of what I was about to do. Had it been only an hour earlier that I had innocently studied their formation?

The coach pulled into the curb of what some might call a quaint street. We were the only people to get off and the coach driver gave me a knowing and disapproving look when he handed me my suitcase. He knew full well that I was headed for Bath. When the bus pulled away, taking with it my change of mind, we were left to face each other.

Standing, my stranger was taller and leaner than I had thought. Face on, without the red vinyl backdrop of the bus seats, he was less robust and less self-assured. A drizzling mist descended on us and seemed to wash away our pretentions. He, too, was looking at me as though he had just seen me. I could feel my hair beginning to flatten around my face in a manner that my mother would call "unbecoming".

Elliot reached and cupped my chin.

"OK?"

In my peripheral vision, there was nothing but grey, and I thought of another time when I stood with a man in the rain, and we felt like the only people alive.

"This way," he said, picking up my suitcase and pausing to consider the non-existent traffic before crossing the street.

I walked a few steps behind him, I wondered why the bus had dropped us so far out of town, until I noticed that we were in its heart. Avebury looked as though it had lost itself – a scattering of shops and houses with no plan. The buildings were drained of colour and looked surprisingly dusty on such a dank day. Several cars were parked in the main street but otherwise, the only life to be seen was a few sheep grazing near the road behind a barbed-wire fence. Elliot must have read my thoughts; he turned to me and grimaced.

"It doesn't get much better, I'm afraid."

I shrugged as if it didn't matter, as if I were free-spirited and adaptable. But that was Madeleine. I placed my hand over the pocket in my bag, reminding myself of why I was there.

We walked on. Not far into the street Elliot paused outside a double-storey red-brick building without character or signage.

"This is it," he said, and gave me a wink before opening the heavy oak door.

I disliked winks; they always seemed so full of suggestion of something I didn't quite understand. I thought of how my mother would sometimes wink at me over my father's shoulder when he embraced her, as if she and I were in some way conspirators against him.

Inside, the foyer and reception were a surprise. Despite the dowdy exterior, the interior was modern and light. Instead of the worn, floral Westminster I was expecting, floorboards shone with their lacquer and gave a honeyed glow to the bare white walls. No large vase of dried flowers on the reception desk. Instead, the polished Oregon wood of its counter held only a small temple bell that sat at its centre.

Elliot placed the bags on the floor. When he lifted the bell, its chime bounced around the walls and floor. From behind the alcove that surrounded the desk, a tiny grey-haired woman stepped forward. When she saw Elliot, her face beamed with pleasure.

"Welcome back!" she said, with genuine delight.

He reached across the counter and took her hand.

"Hello, Mabel. My word, you're looking frisky."

Mabel laughed; the tinkling sound I had expected from the bell.

"Cheeky as ever," she said. "What's brought you here this time?"

I wondered how often Elliot had visited Avebury. What treasures did this inconsequential region hide?

"Now, Mabel," he chided her, "you know I can't tell you."

"We'll see, when you've had a glass or two, how your tongue will wag."

Mabel's eyes shifted to mine.

"Hello, dear."

Elliot turned suddenly as if he'd forgotten that I was behind him.

"I am sorry. Mabel, this is Dana, a business colleague from Australia. I'm afraid I'll need an extra room this time."

"Hello... welcome to our beautiful neck of the woods."

I had only remembered denuded fields and miserable sheep grazing. I stepped forward.

"Hello, Mabel... Yes, it's lovely."

She turned her gaze back to Elliot. "Well, this must be an important trip," she said, turning to a computer screen that had been obscured by the desk. "Two singles, is it?"

I noticed that her hand shook with the Parkinson's rattle as she plucked at the keyboard.

"You're in luck," she said, hitting enter to confirm our place. This B&B was apparently in demand.

"Rooms 9 and 10. You'll know the way, Elliot."

I followed him to a narrow flight of stairs that angled away from the foyer. Its wood was older than the floor below, but richly polished and a deep burgundy and black runner buffered the sounds of our inelegant lumbering. On a small landing, Elliot paused to wait for me.

"Gorgeous, isn't she? But don't let that guise fool you. Mabel is truly a Miss Marple – on to everything. I'm sure she'll grill me about you at some point."

"She's probably used to you." I avoided looking at him.

"I see." It was said with good humour. "You think I come all the way to Avebury for trysts? Believe me, I can find better places."

We continued up the stairs.

That's not my business, I said to myself.

The runner divided left and right along a corridor where the minimalist theme continued. Outside the gloss-white door of room nine, Elliot waited with my bag. Despite my protests, he insisted on taking it inside "to check" that everything was in order. When I opened the door, I was greeted with a blast of colour and patterns. The effect was shocking, and I gasped.

"Oh dear, "Elliot laughed, "I forgot to warn you."

We stepped into the 1950s. It seemed that everything I'd expected to find in the foyer was crowded into this room.

"Are they all like this?" I blinked away a potential migraine from the clash of patterns – red, green and white floral carpet and wallpaper covered in diamond shapes whose monotony was broken only by the different pastel shades of bouquets at their centre. A single bed draped in a pink candlewick bedspread took up most of the room. A doll dressed in a white Terylene tutu sat at its centre.

Elliot placed my bag on the floor. He led me back to the corridor and, outside 10, paused before unlocking it to give me a "ready?" look. I stood in the doorway, stunned. Though the white walls had been continued here, they were framed with a heavy border of royal blue and gold. By the window and facing the door was a large brass and blue statue of Tutankhamen. From the doorway I could see the bathroom where brass taps overhung a marble basin. A large, gilded mirror reflected my astonishment and Elliot's amusement. For an instant I took us in. We didn't "match" and the effect was sobering.

"Are they all themed?" I asked, turning to leave.

"I haven't been here that often to know, but I suspect so. For some reason, Mabel thinks this room suits me."

I glanced again at his reflection and shifted my eyes to King Tut. Yes, I thought, I can see that.

"I think she means regarding my work with antiquities."

Caught out I could feel myself reddening. I turned a sharp angle and nearly knocked over an oversized ceramic black cat that sat regally on its haunches by the door. Its jade-green eyes held a lazy disdain, but I was drawn to the slit of its pupils. A rush of blood momentarily distorted my perception and it seemed that the pupils dilated slightly, drawing me into their blackness.

"Steady." Elliot clasped me around my shoulders. "Though the effect is giddying, I have to admit I quite like it."

In the corridor, I made my excuse to leave. I was weary and my head was clouded as if I was about to get a migraine. He apologised that he had to keep his appointment, but that he would contact his friend in Glastonbury, and recommended the tearoom three doors along the street for lunch.

"There's only the local hotel for a meal tonight, I'm afraid. See you at seven? Will you be all right for the afternoon?"

I didn't hesitate to answer affirmatively and was already considering the cost of a taxi to Bath in his absence.

In my room I lay on the sagging bed cloaked in rose-pink candlewick. The effect was comforting, like being cradled in my mother's mohair coat, though I couldn't actually remember her doing that. It must have been my aunt, who always seemed to be hungry for us. The two women were so different, and I wondered who they resembled. My grandparents, who had emigrated from Sussex, had died long before I was born, and the few anecdotes told created an ill-fitting composite of them. The only photograph of my grandmother was of a severe-looking girl dressed in white lace. I remember that her eyes were dark and sad as though she was not comfortable in front of the camera. A nervous woman, my mother would say of her, frightened by storms, electricity, and her six children. She was superstitious, suffered migraines and sought relief in Chinese herbalists; her proud British gentility hiding an abiding interest in the occult.

From my cosy wrap, I took in the details of the room. The bed faced the window that sparkled with Mabel's pride, though small smudges along its rim gave away her failing eyesight. Heavy drapes in rose-red and ivory stripes had no dust in their folds, unlike those I'd seen in more expensive hotels. The diamond wallpaper was smooth, and each panel matched the next in perfect precision so that it was difficult to find the joins. Along the skirting board, wear and tear had been patched and repainted in gloss paint that highlighted the occasional white rose in the carpet.

On the wall to the right of the bed was a winter painting of the Pantheon in the Stourhead Gardens. I had seen its sunny representations many times, but the one I remembered the most was a tapestry that hung on the dining room wall of my aunt's home. As a child, that room had made me melancholy because I knew that my grandparents had each been laid out there in death. The tapestry became to me a mausoleum in an idealised English after-life. I looked away, but my eyes were drawn back to it again. I pulled the bedspread around me, tucking in my arms and drawing it up around my chin until it enveloped me like a shroud.

Under a single ray of painted sunlight, the Pantheon's dome shone like the crown of a skull and reflected the light on the steps that led to its pillared entrance. The gardens and lake surrounding it were covered in snow and mounded beneath the bare-limbed trees. On the steps was a small black mark that spoiled the painting's pristine beauty. From the bed, it looked like a speck of dirt, but, as I focussed on it, it moved. A fly, I thought, but it seemed to be slowly ascending, pausing before each step. I threw off the quilt and stumbled over my shoe as I went to look more closely; the "fly" had gone. The door to the Pantheon was ajar and inside, revealed through a thin stroke of the painter's brush, was dark and threatening. I returned to the bed and rolled away from the painting towards the clock. Half past one. Though it was getting late for lunch, I could already feel the shutdown stages of sleep approaching.

In my dream, I ascended the steps of the Stourhead Pantheon, but my legs were weak and frail. When I looked at the skin on the backs of my hands it was withered and grey and was shedding along my arms. To my right, I could sense the presence of a companion and turned to see the black cat with jade eyes stepping, and pausing, stepping, and pausing, always one pace behind me. It didn't seem to fear me but willed me to go ahead. I, too, paused and turned to the scene around me. Snow lay like icing on a hurriedly turned cake. Farms were abandoned to the cold and desolation. Though my own blood ran coldly in my veins, my heart was burning with sorrow and grief. I had lost someone. I turned again to the steps and mounted them painfully, the cat now rubbing itself against my leg to urge me on. At the door, the interior was black and cavernous. I did not want to enter but lowered myself with effort on to the cold marble balcony. My companion sat on its haunches and closed its eyes. Together, we waited.

CHAPTER TWENTY-EIGHT

A guttural sound in my throat woke me and I couldn't for a moment determine where I was. The clock read three o'clock. In a half-sleep, my dream replayed itself in staccato. I turned to look at the painting and could not shake the sense of loss. Sluggishly, I rose and washed in the small bathroom that consisted of a green porcelain handbasin, a small, green claw-footed bath and toilet with dark wooden seat. In the oval, gilt-edged mirror above the basin, my face was puffy and pallid. Already I had lost the tanned and bright-eyed health of Kos and Rome. Without lunch, I felt lightheaded and decided that I should eat.

There was no sound from room 10 as I passed, and I wondered if I should take the chance to leave. But I was not a prisoner and Elliot could not be made the villain. No Mabel at the desk as I left. Once in the street, I found the tearoom Elliot had suggested. Lace curtains surrounded French-paned windows and door, and a bell announced my entrance. A woman in late middle age, a blur of hyacinth from hair to slippers, appeared from behind the counter. She could have been Mabel's younger sister.

"Hello, dear, what can I do for you? I'm afraid there's not much left."

I went over to the glass cabinet that housed two vanilla slices, a happy-face biscuit, and three dry-looking scones.

"Just tea, please... and a scone."

"Is that an Australian accent I hear, dear?"

I smiled.

"I've met a few of you in these parts," she said, sliding the glass pane and extracting a sorry scone with tongs.

My head began to spin, and I sat down at the closest table.

"It's the stones, dear."

I jerked my head from my hand. "The stones?" My heart was beating loudly.

"Yes, the Avebury Stones. You must know about them. Can't think of any other reason for you to be here," she said, with a laugh as she disappeared behind a plastic strip curtain.

Moments later, she reappeared with a tray, and took great care in putting teapot, cup and saucer on the table.

"You look sad, dear," she said, placing a china plate in front of me. The scone, surrounded by jam and cream, looked happier than it had in the cabinet. "Can I help?"

Her gentle voice and manner, and the way her hand-knitted cardigan pulled tightly across her breasts reminded me of my aunt. Part of me longed to nestle my head into that sea of mauve, to feel the beat and warmth of another woman's heart. She placed a wrinkled hand on my forearm.

"It's never as bad as it seems, dear... This, too, shall pass."

Her words reminded me of Sophia, of her gentle wisdom, and I wondered what grief this woman had faced. I looked at the wedding ring on the hand that still rested on my arm. Its gold was dulled with the tiny scratches of age and seemed to be disappearing into the folds of her finger. Her husband is dead, I thought.

The bell on the door rang behind me and she left to attend to a new customer, patting my shoulder as she went. I poured real tea into the Royal Doulton cup, but there was no strainer. "Hyacinth" was deep in conversation outside in the street, so I let the tea settle and prodded the scone with the knife. When I opened it, its heart was moist and gave off a warm, doughy smell that made me think of Sophia's kitchen and the scones that the Nucleus had baked in my honour. My phone vibrated in my bag.

"Hi Mads."

"How's Bath? Dee?"

With some shame, I realised that I might be a good liar as I launched into anecdotes about my arrival in Bath, and the interior of my hotel room, based on Number Nine.

"What about you?" I was eager to deflect the focus. "How's Paris?"

"Everything's great... but I miss you."

"You don't need to say that. Just be in love and I'll see you in a few days."

"Actually, Carlo and I thought we might come to you..."

"To Bath?" I could feel the pulse in my throat.

"Well, if that's OK with you. Neither of us has been there."

"But I wouldn't have time to spend with you... and..."

"You don't need to. We'll just tour around the area while you're at lectures and meet for dinner."

I tried to reassure myself that I had every right to change my plans if I wanted to, but that only sent me into a deeper state of panic.

"OK... that would be great. When are you coming?"

"Tomorrow evening, about six."

"Tomorrow!"

There was a pause at the other end before my sister's voice returned, both plaintive and reprimanding. "You don't want us to come."

"I do, I do..." I was tripping over my own guilt. "It will be great to see you there... here."

"I'll call you when we're on our way from the airport. See you then."

"Lovely... can't wait. See you, Mads."

God! I internally roared to my scone and clicked off the phone. I strained the last of the tea between my teeth and could have bitten the side of the cup. Hyacinth had returned and moved her mauve haze into my vision.

"Can I sit for moment, dear?"

My teeth edged off the cup's rim and I placed it delicately on its saucer. "Of course."

Hyacinth looked at the inoffensive cup. "Oh dear." She picked it up and placed it face down on the saucer and turned it as Sophia and my aunt had done.

From the tarnished silver chain around her neck, she lifted spectacles to her eyes, then studied the placement of leaves in the curved inside of the cup. Her lips pursed slightly, and a furrow formed on her brow.

"What is it?" I said, to her powder-blue lids.

"Death," she said, and looked up. Her eyes were not sad, but tranquil. "It comes to us all... in one form or other." She turned the cup a semicircle, "There's a man who waits at the door."

"What door?"

Hyacinth replaced the cup and lifted her spectacles from her nose. "I don't know, dear," she said, fingering the chain at her neck. Her expression was still calm, though distant as if she had forgotten what she had just told me. She smiled, patted my arm again and rose to go about her business. At the plastic curtain, she turned to me.

"Be careful, dear."

Superstitious rubbish, I thought as she disappeared. I slid the phone into my bag and left enough money to cover the tea and consultation. At the door, I paused, hoping that Hyacinth would return with the smiley-face biscuit for consolation, but there was no sign of her.

In the street, I wondered how to kill the few hours before meeting Elliot. With fewer than a dozen shops, it would test my inventiveness. Directly across was a sign with an arrow pointing right to the Avebury Stones. I crossed and followed the direction, passing a butcher's window resplendent in its fake grass, a small bakery where the odour of warm yeast seeped through the pores of its brick façade, and the inn where Elliot and I would dine later. Unlike the country hotels at home there was no deep verandah with loose or missing wrought iron filigree. The double-storey fascia was bare except for a string of fairy globes and had been recently painted white; tiny drops of dry paint peppered the footpath in front. A swinging sign identified it rather unambitiously as the Avebury Inn.

As I walked on, I had a different perspective of Hyacinth's tearoom – paint peeled from the external walls and the window frames were in need of repair. Behind the glass, I could just make out the mauve haze as the Holland blind was pulled down. I imagined her retiring to a solitary life behind the plastic strips, to a slice of Madeira cake and tea. Did she look for life's meaning in the bottom of her cup? Further down the street, the road tapered in. The shops here were smaller and two were separated by a cottage turned into a B&B more welcoming than the exterior of our own. I was glad we weren't staying in it – too intimate, and I would never pass as a "business colleague".

At the end of the shopping strip where the town ran out of confidence stood a stone monolith. I came upon it so suddenly that I was momentarily fixed to the spot. Angled in a vertical plane it would have once pointed to the heavens but was now worn by a thousand years of wind and rain. Under the overcast sky, it was a sombre figure and, as I approached, I was aware that I was walking on the balls of my feet. There was a plaque formally identifying this as one of the Avebury Stones, but the rock's imposing presence demanded something less trite. Unlike Stonehenge, I was able to touch it and my fingers caressed it as they had at the Asklepion and at the altar to Minerva.

The road snaked on across flat, green fields that spread broadly towards the hills in the distance. A hundred metres or so further on, a second stone could be seen to the left of the road and, with eyes straining, I could just make out a third. These stones, like Stonehenge, formed a circle. I followed along the informal track created by the feet of pilgrims and wondered about those feet across the years – barefooted, sandalled and clothed in brand-named runners. I wondered, too, why pilgrims came – for curiosity? for salvation? Or simply because the stones called them as they did to me now.

I hadn't anticipated the sun dipping so soon behind the distant hills. Halfway between the second and third stones, I found myself in a twilight world of gunmetal grey. Even the roadside herbs that had cheered me along the way looked melancholy now. The third stone waited. I hurried along the path and when I reached it, stood in its long, blurring shadow. It was taller than the others, more regular, more regal. I sat on the small outcrop at its base with my back against its cold stone.

After the rattle of Rome, the dense silence that hung over the fields was difficult to adjust to. As I sat, I was aware of my mind shouting its random thoughts. That was why I preferred cities, I decided; they helped to block out the internal noise. With the hills and fields behind me, I looked into the epicentre of the circle. From this position, I faced the town and could see there were more houses at its rear. Here and there, lights were being turned on; life was happening in those homes.

I thought of Hyacinth and Mabel and guessed that even if they did live alone, they had their place and their memories. I thought of my parents still in our family home; of my mother dusting around the memorabilia of a life lived in the glow of my father's love; of Madeleine creating her own beauty, as she always had and, with a gripping of my heart, I thought of Julian perhaps now making a life with someone else. And here I was sitting at the feet of a cold stone in a foreign field watching their lives. But, I reminded myself, there is a man in those lights who will be waiting for me tonight and we will talk about the day and, whatever follows, does.

The stone at my back suddenly became warm and I turned quickly. In the light that was left, the darker grains of the rock were apparent. When I looked more closely, I could just make out three letters at eye level: "S", then "U", but the third was becoming lost in the shadows.

"Sooool." I thought I heard it on the wind that now wrapped around my ears, though there was no movement in the grass at my feet. I remembered the lips of the woman in my dream forming the word and looked again at the grains; "L" now stood out clearly.

SUL, SUL, I repeated the word over and over, but it made no sense to me. At that moment, I doubled over as my lower abdomen was gripped with a deep and spreading cramp. My period had finished a week earlier but I checked my underpants for spotting. When I tried to get up the pain hit me in a wave, and I sat down again. My hand searched for my phone but as it started up, the pain subsided. One missed call.

"Dee." My sister's voice was a mixture of irritation and concern. "Where are you!"

I stood up, stiff from the cold and began walking back the way I'd come, free from pain in my abdomen but winded. Though I didn't want to return her call, I knew the longer I delayed, the worse it would be.

"Thank God!" she said immediately, "Where the hell are you?"

"In Avebury."

"Where? You didn't say that earlier... what's going on?"

I was surprised that she was so incensed and wondered if Carlo was beside her, pacing around in circles and goading her on. My mind became scrambled with half-truths. I told her about Elliot, though he became older and doddery in my description, the contact in Glastonbury and the possibility of solving the riddle of the third note. I didn't tell her that I was now walking in near dark, alone in empty fields. I tried to quicken my pace.

"When do you plan to be in Bath, then?" she said in a clipped tone too similar to our mother's.

"Tomorrow evening... to meet you."

"What about the conference?"

"I'll get there."

She must have heard the intended finality in my tone. "OK," she said more gently, "see you there." She clicked off.

I hurried towards the lights of the town. Under the first streetlamp, I checked the time. I had been in the fields for four hours and had only 30 minutes before meeting Elliot. As I passed the desk, Mabel was sitting at the computer. Highlighted under modern down lights her hair was a white halo. Without looking up she spoke softly: "Have a nice day, dear?"

I stopped, breathless from the walk.

"Mabel, is the woman in the tearoom your sister?"

Her mouth pursed, as Hyacinth's had, but in disapproval rather than concentration. She gave a small sniff and jerk of her head. "Yes," she said, still not looking at me and clicked the mouse of her computer with finality.

As I went up the stairs, I could hear her long, irritated sigh.

A golden light seeped from the base of Elliot's door, and I hurried past.

CHAPTER TWENTY-NINE

Once showered and dressed, I considered myself in the long mirror on the back of the door and was glad that I didn't have many clothing choices; nothing was going to look good enough, I thought as I picked and pulled at the hem of the black jersey dress.

I sat on the bed to pull on black tights when I felt the cramping begin in a deep point of my abdomen, then spread in a surge that felt as if something was being stretched. It was quicker than before and less intense. In the bathroom I checked my underpants again; no sign of a period but the tights felt uncomfortable around my waist, and I pulled them off. Back in the bedroom, I lay on the bed and prodded my abdomen looking for swellings and reminding myself that I'd had a full medical examination only a month earlier, but there were some worrying symptoms.

When the pain subsided, I put on black heels and quickly filled my clutch bag with credit card, cash, lip gloss and comb, and grabbed my new blue jacket as I left. Elliot was preparing to knock when I opened the door and was wide-eyed with surprise.

"Hellooo," he said, with an appreciative grin and took me in with that slow sweep of the eyes. "Splendid."

He was fresh-faced and pink from the shower and smelled of soap and a subtle cologne. The perfectly pressed business shirt had been replaced with a royal-blue polo that set off his Nordic eyes to a stunning effect, even in the dull light of the corridor. He knew it.

"Ready?" he said, reaching out to take my hand. I clasped it uncertainly and pulled the door behind me, realising, as I did, that I had left the key inside.

Mabel was not at the desk. In the cool air outside, Elliot took my jacket and draped it around my shoulders. Facing me, he pulled it gently over my breasts. I looked away.

"I don't bite," he said with a laugh. "Well, not too hard."

"How was your day?" I said, accepting the crook of his elbow. As we walked across the street, I imagined Mabel at the window. Business colleague indeed.

On the other side of the street, Elliot pivoted on his heel to answer my question. "Ahhh... I have some persuading to do."

He'd be good at that, I thought. "Did you see it? The votive?"

"Oh yes... a real treasure... beautiful." His tone was soft, and I was impressed with what seemed to be genuine appreciation of the artifacts he dealt in.

"I would love to see it."

"You will... tomorrow."

We passed the butcher's, with its red blind rolled down

signalling the end of the day; the bakery was cold and odourless. Where the inn had looked drab during the day, it now glittered with the fairy lights that framed the building. The one window that looked on to the street glowed from the muted lighting inside. Outside, two men were leaning on a bench drinking ale from large jugs and laughing. Although I'd never been a part of the pub culture in Australia, I now wanted to find, inside this hotel, a motley collection of locals taking up their respective positions around the bar, and an amiable publican who might, as he came to the punch line of his joke, slap the counter in welcome when he saw us come in. But there was no one at the bar and a stern-faced waitress looked up as we entered a very red dining room. Without speaking, she picked up menus from the station and led us towards a table by the wall. As she walked ahead, I took in her crisp, if not starchy, white shirt and a black skirt that sat too snugly over her buttocks and caused her to walk rigidly. A colloquial Australian saying came to mind.

There had been some attempt, in the past, to give this room a look of opulence, but the red flocked wallpaper was beginning to peel along its joins, and several globes had blown in the larger-than-necessary chandelier that hung precariously above a table for four. Each setting included a small candle nestled in a ruby glass holder. The rosy glow helped to flatter skin tones and I wondered if it helped to disguise stubborn stains on the stiff white tablecloths.

Elliot's order for pinot noir was taken before I could speak. Irritated, I picked up a menu.

"Will you be ordering my meal as well?"

He looked bewildered and embarrassed. I remembered that I had made Julian look that way more than once, and he had been far less deserving.

"I'm sorry," I said, and meant it.

In the candlelight, Elliot's eyes looked innocent and soft. "No need. Is there anything you would prefer to drink?"

"No, a red would be nice," I said. It was my due to be embarrassed.

When it was brought to the table, I noted the Yarra Valley label. Elliot sampled and poured my wine with a glance that shifted from the glass to my face, as if he was administering the elixir of life. The soft clink of our glasses in meeting was like a kiss and I sipped with pleasure, remembering the previous night when I had sat in a different restaurant with my sister and her lover. The couple beneath the cornucopia came to mind, the sparkle of the champagne and her eyes. In my own glass, light seemed to have disappeared.

"What did you do with your day?" he said.

The simple domesticity of the question caught my breath, though I couldn't tell if his interest was genuine. I told him about Hyacinth, and about the Avebury Stones, but I didn't speak of how I thought the grains of rock spelt out "SUL", or how I had imagined that the wind whispered it to my ears.

"My sister will be meeting me in Bath tomorrow evening."

Elliot's face had been impassive, but it was now bewildered.

"I thought you might... that we might... stay on in Glaston-bury and..."

"I'm on my way to a conference, Elliot. When we've met with your contact tomorrow, I'll have to go. What time are we to meet him?"

"Eleven o'clock," he said to the flocked wallpaper, then sipped his wine. When he replaced the glass, he spoke to his fingers in a monotone. "I pick the piece up at nine."

"You can take it?" I said, feeling a hot thrill run through my body. "I thought you would just copy the inscription..."

"Yes, it's not unusual. I need to authenticate it before I buy."

He had met my eye and suddenly I was aware that he was as lonely as I was. I resisted the impulse to reach out and touch his hand, aware of the beguilement of candlelight, wine and attentive company. "Tell me about it."

When he spoke about seeing the votive offering for the first time, he became animated, and blood ran in its enthusiasm to his face. "I'm certain it's authentic. It's just a matter of having proof – for resale purposes."

"Do you find it difficult to part with some of the treasures you've come across?"

"At first, but you don't make money that way. I've held on to some favourites, though."

"What sort of things?"

He considered before answering. "An odd collection, actually, that has more aesthetic appeal than monetary value. There's an Egyptian scarab that was found at the site of a recent dig,"

I thought of my own, lying in the jewellery box at home.

"Because they're quite common, it's not worth a great deal, but at the time I came across it, I was going through a difficult period and... it just seemed to cheer me."

I noticed that he became subdued, but we were interrupted by the waitress.

While he ordered his meal, I considered what he had said. "A difficult period... and recently."

The waitress tottered away.

"Are you all right now?" I asked.

He paused, "Oh... yes, I think so. A breakup – it happens."

"How long were you together?"

"Six years."

I noticed that he was lightly tapping the tablecloth with the middle finger of the hand that rested on the table. Without prompting, I told him then about Julian, his transfer to London, and our separation.

"You couldn't maintain a distant relationship?"

His question stabbed at my heart and my conscience. Julian's words echoed. The irony was that I had thought that it would be impossible to sustain it, yet here I was only an hour's drive from him.

"You're not over him," Elliot said quietly.

I could feel hot tears ready to flow but dug my thumbnail into the palm of my hand. I couldn't speak. He raised his glass and offered a toast. "It seems we have more in common than we thought."

Over venison and field mushrooms, I learned that Elliot was from a middle-class background and that he had been awarded a scholarship to study history at Cambridge. I asked him why he'd become interested in antiquities. He coloured.

"My grandmother's brooch. I know, it hardly belongs in the antiquity category, but when I was seven, she gave it to me and asked me to take care of it. I was a serious young boy, and I did just that. It was silver and sparkled with marcasite. I thought it must have been worth a fortune, but it was, of course, just costume jewellery. She lived alone in a rented second storey of a house in Knightsbridge. Mostly it was one large living room, but it was enchanting. The wooden floors always seemed to have been freshly polished and the soft smell of floor wax has remained a favourite scent for me. There was a large rug that took up most of the floor space. It was royal blue and gold and, though I can't quite remember the design, I don't think I've ever seen one quite the same, or as beautiful," he mused. "My grandmother was a minimalist." He looked away for a moment, lost in his memory and I noted that his ears were perfectly shaped. "Though I doubt she would have called herself that. There were few ornaments and, years after she died, I discovered that those I thought were made of gold were just brass." He took a sip and his lips rested on the edge of the glass. He moved them away slowly, seductively, "A bit like the brooch, not quite the real thing. But what I loved about it all, what I loved about my grandmother, was her capacity to create beauty out of the ordinary."

"Yes," I said, thinking of Madeleine's and Sophia's gardens, and my tiny scone with its scoured leaves made in Sophia's kitchen. "And yet your work deals with the truly authentic. I'm sure you'd be unhappy if you had been duped by the beauty of a fake!"

"Very true, but I think my grandmother's legacy was to give me an eye, an appreciation for beauty." He paused and the air between us seemed to be heated by more than the candle.

I buttered a piece of bread I had no hunger for.

He continued, "My grandmother came from another era, and the brooch was my connection to it. I feel that way about all the pieces I come across. When I hold or see one for the first time, it's like I've been catapulted back into another time." He looked down at the flame between us, breaking the connection of our eyes. His brow slightly furrowed, and I was able to imagine the serious young boy wrapping the brooch in a silken handkerchief and storing it, tenderly, at the back of a drawer.

"What about you?" he said gently as he looked up. "Why obstetrics?"

I opened my mouth to give the standard response to the question I'd been asked many times, but I couldn't remember what I would have said.

"You wanted to change the world?" he prompted.

"Something like that. Certainly, I wanted to make a difference... to be there at the moment of birth... to ensure that all babies, and their mothers in my care, survived, and experienced a positive and life-affirming moment."

In my mind Bonnie's lids flew open and her eyes rolled upwards as her body began to arch on the bed. I felt her gasp for air caught in my own chest. My hand shook as I brushed a hair from my eye. Without speaking he reached across the table and rested his palm on my other hand. I felt cold and began to tremble. The candle on the table quivered in my exhalation. Elliot lightly squeezed my hand in support.

"It still happens in the West. Mothers and babies die. Had it never happened to you before?"

"Yes, there had been two others. One was a baby with serious defects, and, in the end, it was a blessing, and the other was a woman with a history of chronic heart disease who had been warned against becoming pregnant but did. There was nothing wrong with Bonnie beforehand. It was unexpected."

"What did the autopsy find?"

"Cardiac arrest brought on by preeclampsia."

"You were exonerated?"

"Yes." I could still see the husband's haunted look when the verdict was handed down. A woman standing next to him was holding a young baby who cried in her arms. When she looked up at me, her eyes filled with grief. She was holding Bonnie's baby.

Elliot savoured his wine and took me in. "You must forgive yourself, Dana," he said, pouring me another glass.

In the glow of the candle, the wine was the colour of pomegranate juice, lit from within by its own life force. I sipped and felt the energy of it run into my veins. The muscles in my shoulders began to slacken and the face of this "stranger" became familiar and comforting.

"You are a beautiful woman," he whispered across the rim of his glass. Feathery lashes fanned his eyes in hypnotic, slow movements. He leaned closer. The flickering light beneath his chin cast deep shadows around his eyes and the scars of his adolescence formed a lunar landscape.

As my own gaze lingered on his lips, I felt as though I was caught in a page of a romantic novel. Would he cup the back of my head with one hand and draw me to his lips? The warm pleasure of my arousal took me by surprise.

"Should we retire for the night?" he said, drawing back from the flame and I smiled inwardly at the expression.

Mechanically, I collected my bag and jacket as the waitress returned with the receipt. As we stepped into the street, he again placed the jacket around my shoulders and threaded my arm in the crook of his. When we walked, we had to readjust our pace to synchronise, and it occurred to me that Julian and I had always been in step. I shook off the thought and pressed my hand into Elliot's arm searching for the muscle beneath his shirt. He flexed and drew my hand in closer.

Though it was early, Mabel had already locked the front door. Elliot produced a key, and I was irritated that I hadn't been offered one of my own. I remembered, then, that I'd left the key in my room. Perhaps Mabel had given Elliot the master key.

"You can't get into your room? What a shame."

At the top of the stairs, I turned quickly to catch his expression, but his face was deadpan. He headed for my door and, with his back to me, wrestled with the handle.

"I'm afraid you are locked out."

"What about Mabel? She lives here somewhere, doesn't she?"

"I have no idea," he said smoothly, "I've never had to look. You'll have to come in."

Embarrassed, but still feeling languid from the wine, I took a step towards him and softly tapped his chest with my fists.

We laughed and he drew a protective arm around me. "I like it," he said, guiding me towards his door.

Elliot closed the door and slipped the jacket from my shoulders. Before I could move, his hands ran up my arms and gently kneaded their muscles. He stepped closer and, when I felt his warm breath in my hair, then on the nape of my neck, I leaned back into him. A soap-opera came unbidden into my mind, though the reality was more awkward than the slick seduction scenes I had witnessed. In truth they had provided me with some distraction on lonely afternoons of recent months.

When his hands slipped through my arms, I was startled. When I turned, his lips were parting. The wine had stained the inside of his mouth so that it formed a deep chasm and a flickering bulb outside the window captured the hypnotic movement of his tongue in rapid still frames. With my breath suspended, I moved towards it, parting my lips to receive it. There was urgency, and a violence in that kiss and I dipped and withdrew with pleasure and repulsion.

CHAPTER THIRTY

I n the morning, I woke to the pressure of Elliot's arm across my waist. I slipped from beneath its dead weight, careful not to wake him, and went into the bathroom. In the mirror my eyes were light-lidded and bright, and colour had returned to my cheeks in an oestrogen-fed bloom. For a moment I wondered if we had consummated the passion of the previous night, but remembered the abdominal cramp, and Elliot's concern. He lay now deep in sleep and had experienced an angelic conversion in the steady morning light.

The bedside clock read half past seven, and I wondered if Mabel was already at the desk. My dress was crushed beneath the blankets and, when I slipped it on, I made a feeble attempt to straighten it. Mabel would not be fooled. From under the bed, I retrieved my bag and shoes, stepped defiantly past the ceramic Abyssinian cat, and closed the door behind me. When I tried the door handle to my own room it opened with ease. Under the shower, I let the water run down the length of my spine while I prodded at my abdomen, pressing under the rib cage toward the liver, and down into the pit of my groin. There was no sensitivity and I felt better than I had in a while.

I dressed slowly, thinking about Elliot and wondering how he would be this morning. When I'd packed my suitcase, I checked the phone. One missed call – Julian. My fingers fumbled as I retrieved the message, and my hand was unsteady as I brought it to my ear.

"Dana... it's Julian."

There was a pause.

"I'm just calling... to see how you are."

Another pause.

"Dana..." His voice was soft and plaintive, and I waited.

"I'll try you again later."

I replayed the message, listening to his tone, and even more to the silences, but it told me nothing. The cramp returned and I lay on the bed and closed my eyes.

"Dana... Dana...." Julian was calling me, and I was searching rooms in a dark and cavernous house guided only by the sound of his tapping. Door after door was opened, but inside were only windowless rooms and sinister, dark recesses. His tapping became more urgent, and I scrambled along slippery corridors towards a crack of light that seemed to be angled at a height above me. As I came closer the tone of his voice changed.

"Dana... Dana...." I rushed to the door of my 1950's room, stumbling over my bag in a sleep-induced haze. Elliot was standing on the other side.

"Are you all right?"

"Yes, thanks." I tried to hide my disappointment and gathered my things.

He didn't mention the previous evening, and neither did I. At the desk, Mabel was polishing the counter with vigour. When she looked up, she greeted Elliot with a smile.

"You're up early. So ... when will we have the pleasure of your company again?"

"Not for a while, I'm afraid, unless there is something I might be interested in."

She looked beyond him to me and was about to speak but seemed to think better of it. I stepped forward as Elliot was getting out his wallet.

"I'll settle my account too, Mabel," I said.

She looked at him.

Elliot turned to me. "Please Dana, you're here at my invitation. After all, I derailed you."

Mabel flicked at a bit of dust on the counter, her face settling into an expression of amused anticipation while she waited. I tried to decline Elliot's offer, but gave up under his insistence.

"Lovely to meet you, dear," she said when all was settled, and we picked up our bags. "I hope you enjoyed yourself."

In the foggy street, the cab, a black vintage Humber, was waiting. When we had settled into the back, Elliot spoke with the driver, whom he seemed to know, then turned to me while he placed his briefcase at his feet. "Still happy to go?"

"Yes," I said, "definitely."

We still hadn't mentioned the previous night and I wondered if Elliot really believed my physical discomfort. I rested my hand on his arm as way of reassurance and, perhaps, apology. He returned the gesture with a "don't worry about it" pat as the taxi pulled away from the kerb.

The interior of the cab seemed disproportionately large to the outside. The seats were a worn deep-brown leather. A sliding glass pane separated us from the driver, who wore an oversized hat that sat over his ears; I hoped that he could see past its peak. We left Avebury through the main street and along the road I had walked the day before, passing the stones that loomed as ghostly shadows in the mist.

"How far to Glastonbury?" I asked, once we were on the motorway.

"About half an hour," Elliot said.

"Do you have the piece already?" I said, looking at his briefcase.

Carefully, he lifted it to his knees and the clicking of the locks as they opened sounded portentous.

Without a word, he produced a bubble-wrapped package that was small enough to fit in one hand. He returned the brief-case to the floor and rested the parcel on his knees, unwrapping it with the slow care of a loving parent. When he lifted it out, I thought of the moment of presenting a newly born child to its parents. Even the plainest, like this old piece before me, inspired love.

The votive was simple – a woman squatting in childbirth. Elliot offered it to me, and I cupped my hands to receive it, surprised by its weight. The woman's closed eyes and mouth were single lines and years of weathering had worn a smile into the fixed and determined face. Her short, thick body was naked, and her crooked arms and hands were moulded into bent thighs. Between her legs the vulva was swollen around the bulge of a baby's crown. Though the piece was covered in mineralised sediment, her round breasts and vulva shone with the smooth white marble beneath. I ran my thumb over them and imagined a woman, in a distant past, doing the same. When I turned her over, so that she rested face down in my palm, I saw the inscription on her back. It consisted of seven symbols—vertical strokes, semi-formed letters and circles, all of which I recognised from the last of my letters.

"How old do you think?"

Elliot had been quiet beside me and seemed to be lost in his own thoughts. "I'd say circa 800BCE."

"That's older than Hippocrates... as old as Asklepios," I said, thinking aloud. "Who do you think she is?"

"Name your earth goddess." He held out his hand. "There were many back then, but it depends on where this one has come from."

Reluctantly I gave it back. "And you think your contact in Glastonbury will know?"

"Not necessarily, but if he can translate the symbols, it will help." He returned it to the case.

"What's your gut feeling?"

He clicked the locks with finality, and looked at me directly, sadly. "That you're still in love."

I sank back into the seat, not sure what to say. My lips made an effort to deny it but they had lost their energy.

Elliot turned to me, "It's all right, Dana. I know how you feel."

CHAPTER THIRTY-ONE

On the road to Glastonbury, I learned that, for all Elliot's bravado and smooth talk, he was grieving for a woman who, it seemed, no longer cared. I reached for his hand. He accepted mine and, together, we sat in silence for the last 10 minutes of the journey. I was reminded of a schoolyard friend on our first day of school and for the several weeks that followed. Each day we would find each other at lunchtime and hold hands. He became an obnoxious brat not long after and lost interest in me, but I still recalled the comfort we felt in each other as we weathered the storm of our new lives.

The outskirts of Glastonbury were like those of most cities I'd seen. Renovated and neglected homes stood side by side, the former showing the latter what they could be. I had expected to see more young people with dyed hair and alternative clothes, as I might if I was approaching Byron Bay, but there seemed to be mostly middle-aged conservatives.

The heart of the city, on the other hand, was as expected. As our driver followed Elliot's directions, shop after shop displayed their wares in technicolour but, in a relatively quiet lane, Elliot asked the driver to stop. He nodded towards a single-fronted shop with one beautifully upholstered chair in the window. Above the door, a swinging sign read "Under Cover". I was puzzled but, after paying the cabbie, Elliot was holding the door open for me.

We collected our bags from the boot and stood at the shop's door as the cab left. Elliot knocked and, while we waited, I noted the intricate pattern of the chair's fabric, a fine gold leaf set against an olive-green suede. A dead moth lay wedged in the crease of the seat. There was a shuffling sound behind the door and an elderly woman opened it with effort, blinking into the daylight. Her face, framed with wisps of white hair, was heavily lined and hurriedly applied face powder accentuated the pores of her nose and cheeks. When she had adjusted to the light, her irises were small blue cornflowers and, for a moment I wondered if she, too, was a relative of Hyacinth and Mabel. She looked up at Elliot and there was a pause while her neurons fired slowly.

"Hello, Deirdre," he said.

I smiled to myself at the thought that hot-blooded and lustful Elliot seemed to be intimate with a range of elderly ladies.

"Elliot!" There was a singsong lilt of the Welsh in her voice. When she smiled at him, I could see the young girl she had been. Like Mabel, she was slow to register my presence and I wondered if the "inner girl" of both women was still a vibrant flirt.

"Hello," I said, "I'm Dana, Elliot's business colleague." I could feel Elliot's amusement beside me.

"Welcome, Dana," she said, stepping aside with her back to the open door. "Clive is expecting both of you."

Elliot walked purposefully down the narrow corridor, and I followed. In a windowless room lit by a single globe hanging from the ceiling, an elderly man was sitting at the kitchen table. He wore a navy-blue cable-knit jumper, and his white hair was caught in a long, thin ponytail. He seemed to be unaware of our presence and continued to flip through the swatches in the upholstery book in front of him, pausing to record some detail in a school exercise book.

"Clive!" Deirdre's effort to rouse him startled me. "Deaf as a post."

When he looked up, his face was the same shape as hers though the white of his beard and moustache accentuated the blue of his eyes. When he saw Elliot, he slapped the table with pleasure and, with the agility of a younger man, jumped up to greet us. We were introduced and, patting Elliot's arm as he passed him, he gripped my hand.

"Welcome, Dana." And in his beautiful Welsh lilt, I felt that my name had been truly pronounced. "Well, well, you're a beauty," he said. It seemed that Clive's inner man was also a flirt.

"Excuse my brother," Deirdre said from behind me. "He's all talk... or so I'm told."

Clive whooped and squeezed my hand tighter. "Not all talk," he said with a laugh. "She's just asking the wrong women."

He motioned me to a chair at the table. Elliot was already sitting and was watching us with wry amusement while he unlocked the briefcase on his lap. Clive was still chuckling to himself but sobered quickly when he saw the marble woman on the table. He sat down quietly, respectfully and, in answer to his questioning eyebrows, Elliot handed her to him. Deirdre continued to the next room which, from the echoes of her movements on hard surfaces, I assumed was the kitchen.

"Ohhh," Clive held the woman in the palm of one hand and stroked across her marble breasts. Gently he turned her over and felt the rough surface for the inscription. He lifted the spectacles that were hanging around his neck to his nose and the puckered expression of concentration made him look a much older man – a ponytailed Merlin. Without speaking to either of us, he turned to a fresh page in the exercise book and began to reproduce the symbols of the inscription.

Near me, I could sense Elliot's suspension of breath and glanced at him. His face was taut and pale, and under the stark light of the globe, the pockmarks of his skin created shadowed polka dots. I thought of the adolescent Elliot, how he would have dealt with ridicule when his skin was raw. There was an edge to him, of defensiveness and vulnerability under the external smooth, and I wondered if my "rejection" was accepted with adolescent resignation. When Clive had finished transcribing, he placed the woman on the table to face me. Between her legs, the swollen vulva was shadowed and the baby's crown, as smooth as its mother's breasts, shone under the light. He pointed to the first two symbols. "Great Mother," he said, glancing at us over the rim of his glasses. He looked back at the book and pointed to the next symbol – a horizontal waving line. "'Of the waters'... a crude translation on my part." He lifted the spectacles from his nose and left them to hang. "The rest of the inscription is too worn to read, but my guess is that it's a fairly standard invocation."

"How old?" Elliot was leaning forward.

"Circa 800, give or take 100 years either way."

"I knew it!" Elliot was beaming. He was good, I had to admit. When I looked up he smiled at me with childlike pleasure.

"Who is she?" I said to Clive.

"This woman? Just a mother giving birth..."

"Who is the Great Mother of the Waters?"

He considered before he spoke. "It could be Brigid – she

was a major deity at the time – but I think it's more likely Sul... yes, Sul."

Both men heard my gasp. Spittle caught at the back of my throat, and I coughed violently. Elliot was out of his chair patting me on the back while Deirdre returned with a glass of water. Clive hadn't moved but seemed to be assessing me with deep interest. "You're shocked. Why is that? Do you know our Sulis?"

"No." I shook my head as I sipped at the water. "Who is she?"

He didn't seem persuaded and continued to watch me closely. "She's a goddess of the Druids... of healing and fertility, paralleling the Egyptian Isis or the Greek Demeter. Her temple was in Bath, at the spring that was there. The Romans, of course, took over the site for their baths."

Elliot shot me a look and I could see the mental connection he was making. "Do you have the note?" And then to Clive: "The one I mentioned on the phone."

I took the third letter from my bag and slid it across the table towards Clive. His wild eyebrows shot up while he returned the spectacles to the bridge of his nose. He unfolded it and held it at arm's length, his face again pointed in concentration. Deirdre, with a dishcloth still in one hand, stood behind him looking over his shoulder. Both had their heads cocked slightly to the left and, in that moment, I couldn't fail to see that they were twins.

Clive laid the note on the table and flattened it so that we could see where he was pointing.

"Again, we see the reference, 'Great Mother of the Waters... return...' no, 'bring to me,' no, 'bring me to,' I'm not sure but it might be 'new life'. 'Great Mother of the Waters bring me to new life.' An unusual order for a fertility invocation. Usually it would be: 'Bring to me new life.' Perhaps it's a mistake. Where did this come from?"

I shook my head and Elliot filled him in on the story of the letters.

"Whoever wrote this," Clive said, folding the letter, "knows his stuff." He handed it to me. "And you have no idea?"

"None," I said, "and I can't imagine who it could be."

"Someone's trying to tell you something, Dana. The gods are talking to you."

I let out a spontaneous laugh that was too loud, almost manic.

"Call me eccentric, but that's what I believe," he said, leaning towards me, "but then, I do live in Glastonbury." He chuckled and leaned back into his chair, at the same time exchanging a look with his sister.

"But I'm just going to Bath for a conference," I said with not as much conviction as I wanted.

Deirdre smiled and patted me on the shoulder as Hyacinth had as she returned to the kitchen. Clive and Elliot resumed their discussion of the marble woman who squatted between us in what now seemed a stance of ridicule. I tried to convince myself that I was simply on my way to a conference in Bath; Clive could invent all the reasons he liked, but there was nothing more to it than that.

Speculation and unproven theories were surrounding me like a thick fog, and I was beginning to feel agitated. I wanted to throw away the notes. I wanted to dispel the fanciful visions and dreams I'd been having. I wanted to talk about quantitative data; about oxytocin levels and ways of reducing the risks of anaesthesia. I wanted to leave. Suddenly, I longed for the rationality of science. I should be in Bath, I told myself.

Elliot must have sensed my agitation. While Clive was speaking, he placed the woman carefully back into his case and stood. "We must be going," he said. The older man rose effort-lessly, shook his hand and then embraced him.

"Always a pleasure, Elliot." Clive held out his arm to enfold me and I complied. The coarseness and smell of his woollen jumper reminded me of my father, and I lingered briefly in the comfort of his arm. "Don't discount it all," he said, pulling back to look me in the eye. "Sul awaits."

I wanted to dismiss it, but there was an authority about Clive that undermined my rationality. Deirdre returned and was surprised to see that we were leaving. "I was about to make a pot. Won't you stay?"

Elliot took her hand. "We'd love to, but perhaps next time."

"We'd like that." She led the way down the corridor.

As we stepped into the street and turned to say goodbye, brother and sister stood in the doorway. In unison, they raised a hand to wave, then disappeared behind the door.

In the cobbled lane, I turned to Elliot. "Where would I catch a bus to Bath?"

He didn't answer immediately but nodded his head to the right of the lane.

"This way," he said. He wasn't looking at me but was walking ahead, talking over his shoulder. Suddenly he stopped and waited for me to catch up. "Dana, won't you stay?" Those beautiful lashes brushed in slow strokes over his eyes, and, despite the chill of the morning, his face was flushed. For a moment I hesitated.

"I have to go, Elliot."

He stood, looking at his shoes then reached into his jacket. "A cab," he said, bringing out his phone.

I would have argued, but I wanted to leave, and quickly.

We were no further than the end of the lane when the cab from Avebury pulled in.

"Is this your private car?"

He shrugged and smiled as he held the door open. When he didn't get in, I felt a small grip of panic. He leaned in and, holding my chin gently between his fingers, covered my face in soft kisses.

"Thank you," he whispered close to my ear. "Take care of her, Harold," he said to the driver.

I gripped his arm as he withdrew, but my throat had constricted, and I made an inadequate sound of goodbye. When he'd spoken with the driver he returned to my window and made a comical gesture of appeal that made me laugh. As the cab moved off, his smile disappeared, and he turned away suddenly. When I looked back, he was walking away, the crouching woman in his case beside him.

CHAPTER THIRTY-TWO

BATH

The journey from Glastonbury to Bath was unmemorable, although the fields were greener than those of Avebury. I needed a distraction, but the driver was not one for conversation and my meagre attempts were answered with a simple: "Yes, Ma'am." The quiet hum of the engine, the sameness of the scenery intensified my thoughts of Elliot walking away.

Fragments of the previous days revisited: the sibling tension between Hyacinth and Mabel, and I wondered if the same potential existed between Madeleine and me, the pattern repeated with Deirdre and Clive, though perhaps tempered by their different genders; the Stourhead Pantheon and the Abyssinian cat who guarded the door. Small towns passed in hypnotic similarity and led me further into thought. The Avebury stones, like ghosts within the fields interplayed with other images—of "SUL" scratched into stone and whispered in the wind; the crouching woman in childbirth appealing to the Great Mother of the Waters, and the knowing look in Clive's eyes when he translated the note.

Elliot entered the cluster of images and I tried and failed to shutter my mind against him. The brash Elliot of the bus was replaced with a more humbled version, the slow blinking of his lashes interpreted now as vulnerability rather than a con. I remembered, too, how gentle he was when I was gripped with pain and wondered if he was relieved that we didn't make love. In truth, I wasn't sure if I was relieved or not. Although I knew I didn't owe Julian any loyalty now, I still felt that I did.

I closed my eyes and listened to the rhythmic drumming of the tyres on the corrugated bitumen and felt his breath at my ear. "Thank you... thank you," The words replayed but with each repetition, the accent changed until it became Julian's voice, now calling my name.

Next to me, the vibrations of my phone in my bag drew me to the present.

"Julian?"

"Hello, Dana."

Between our suspended breaths, the silence formed a deep chasm.

"How are you," he said finally.

Still, I couldn't speak.

"Dana?"

"I'm fine... and you?"

There was a pause. "Where are you?"

"On my way to Bath."

"Is everything all right?"

I felt a rush of guilt but reminded myself that my life was not his business anymore.

"Yes, why?"

"It's just that..."

I saw it clearly then. "You've been talking to Madeleine."

"Yes. She was concerned..."

My guilt had transformed to mild rage. "She had no right to call you... and, by the way, why are you calling?"

There was silence at the other end until he spoke. "I'm sorry, but I was worried, too. Madeline said you were meant to be in Bath, but..."

I tried to suppress the anger in my voice, "So, did she tell you where I am and why?"

He was silent, then: "Not the whole of it."

"Well, I've finished my business now," I said too quickly, "and I'm on my way to the conference. I'll still be meeting them as planned."

"Dana," Julian said softly, "is everything all right between us?"

I didn't know how to answer him. Elliot had said that I was still in love with Julian. Madeleine had said that he was still in love with me.

"Yes," I said, wondering where we really stood with each other. "Why wouldn't it be? We've both moved on, haven't we?"

The words struck the air discordantly as they tumbled from my mouth.

"I see," Julian said, his voice, in contrast to mine, soft and measured.

"I saw you in Rome," I said.

"In Rome? But..." Suddenly he didn't sound so in control. "Dana... Madeleine has said that you've been... exhausted... and..."

"I saw you in Rome, Julian, with your friends and... that's OK... I'm seeing someone now."

It felt as though every red blood cell rushed to my aid. I breathed my lie deeply.

"He's with you now?"

"No, he has business..." I was becoming enmeshed. "I'll see him after the conference."

"Madeleine didn't mention..."

"I can't see why she would need to."

"No... of course. It's good that you're feeling better now."

Was I feeling better? If Julian thought so, and hung up now, I felt that I would lose my only lifeline, no matter how frayed it was, but I reminded myself that he had a new life, and I didn't want to become an object of his pity.

"Yes, I'm feeling well now. Elliot," I said and, as I spoke the name, I felt that I'd snapped the last thread of that line, "has been wonderful." I was trembling, with lies, with fear and the impending sense of what I was about to lose.

"I'm happy for you, Dana."

Was this a relief for him? Could he shrug me off now and get on with his life? I was stricken and mute, afraid of betraying myself.

"By the way," he said, "I received your letter... thanks."

I'd almost forgotten about the letter. What had I said back then, in Kos? Now it seemed a lifetime ago. It was written before I saw him in Rome, before I knew that he was getting on with his life. "I was in a bad, mental space then, Julian."

"I see."

Again, the abyss. I scanned it for clues to his emotions.

"Well," he said slowly, "I must go. I just wanted to be sure you were OK... and you are, so that's good."

"Yes, I'm fine."

"Goodbye, Dana."

I could feel him drawing away. I wanted to reach through the phone and hold him there.

"Goodbye, Julian."

As I shut down the phone with a trembling hand, I stared at the wrinkled and paling leather of the seat in front.

"Are you all right, Ma'am?" Harold's voice jolted me.

"Yes, thanks... far to go?"

"Not far now, Ma'am, about 20 minutes."

I looked out the window and saw that the land was gently undulating and there was a sense of climbing – into the seven hills of Bath. Scattered within the hills were large, imposing homes, the English equivalent of the Roman villas where Sophia lived, though these appeared to be constructed to capture as much sunlight as possible. Although it was midday, the morning sun was like a vapour that clung softly to the trees and slid easily down the large, double-glazed windows. Behind one I could see the full body of a woman looking out at the hills. She looks lonely, I thought, but almost on cue a man came to stand beside her and looped an arm around her waist. I wanted, then, to go home, to the clarity of the Australian sun and the glaring intensity of its summers, of air that crackled with radiant heat and the crunch of exhausted cicadas lying among eucalyptus twigs beneath my feet.

Twenty minutes later, as promised, we began our descent. Harold crooked his head towards me.

"Bath, Ma'am," he said, and I recognised that he said it with great pride.

Before me the city spread out from a knotted heart along the arteries of roads and into the hills. Even from a distance I could sense Bath's splendour, as if it knew that it was a blessed city.

The Humber descended the hills quietly. The outskirts of the city showed none of the usual signs of a city's decaying, forgotten edges. Along the pavement, a group of school students in immaculate navy-blue-and-white uniforms clustered around a teacher who, by the waving of his arms towards the building in front of them, seemed to be explaining some facet of local architecture. A mother with a baby in an oversized and expensive pram went to skirt around them and I noted how the students respectfully stepped aside to let her pass.

As we came closer to its heart, the homes became smaller and Georgian terraces dominated the streets. The pedestrian and car traffic were much busier and so was its pace.

"Where to, Ma'am?"

I rifled through my bag for the address and told him the name of the guesthouse.

"Yes, Ma'am."

"You know it?"

"It's 'The Knowledge', Ma'am." He touched the peak of his cap with a gloved hand and, in the rear vision mirror I saw the skin concertina around his smile. The analogue clock embedded in the walnut dashboard read 11 o'clock. The conference session was not for an hour, so I had time to check in and freshen up. After the events of the morning, I was looking forward to a scientific discussion. I wondered if Madeleine and Carlo had arrived. Would the nobility of this city irritate the egocentric racing car driver?

The cab pulled up outside a white Georgian-styled guest house that appeared to be centrally located. Harold raised his hand in rejection of the notes I offered.

"Mr Sinclair has looked after it, Ma'am."

I was confused.

"Mr Elliot..." he explained, keeping a poker face.

As I closed the door of the cab, I felt as though I was ending a significant hiatus in my journey, though my fingers retained their grip on the handle. It needn't end here, I thought. He smiled and tapped his cap in farewell. I let go of the door.

CHAPTER THIRTY-THREE

The foyer's interior was spare and modern, and I wondered if I would be greeted by another Mabel. At the desk was a dark-skinned man in his thirties who looked up from the computer screen as I approached. The stark white of his shirt contrasted beautifully with his skin and highlighted the manicured fingernails that slid reluctantly from the keyboard.

"Good morning," he said in Oxford English, flashing brilliant teeth which, I noted, were captivatingly crooked. When I told him my name, he produced a key from the desk and asked me to follow him along the corridor that opened into a large octagonal atrium. As we entered, sunlight blasted from behind a cloud like a spotlight signalling our arrival. The atrium was an extension of the original Georgian building whose rear brick façade was visible through the glass ceiling. It was furnished with tropical colours of red, yellow and green and I half-expected to see a toucan in a cage. Large books on exotic architecture and furnishings were placed for best effect on a glass coffee table. The effect was dazzling and, even though it seemed an incongruous sight in England, in the sun that streamed through the glass, it worked.

To my left, double doors led out to a paved courtyard filled with white wrought-iron tables and chairs. I followed my guide across the room to a corridor that led to an extension of the building. He stopped at the first room on the left and, when he opened the door, again the sun was there to greet me through the single glass door that faced the courtyard.

"Perfect," I said.

He gave a small bow and smiled with pride that made me wonder if he was the owner, the tropical atrium a concession to his homesickness.

"Breakfast is served in the dining room from six o'clock," he said, backing into the corridor. "The Conservatory," he said, gesturing to the glass room, "is open to guests until 11pm." He turned towards the telephone on the modest writing desk behind us. "There is 24-hour attendance at the desk, though the kitchen closes at 10."

I thanked him and inquired about the distance to the university, noticing that my speech had become more rounded in the presence of his perfect English. Only a 10-minute walk, he assured me, and gave the directions. When he had left, I sat on the single bed and wished that I'd allowed myself the luxury of a double room. This time, I was truly on my own. Solitude, I was beginning to realise, was only appealing when there were others waiting for you to return to them, and I now looked forward to my sister's imminent arrival.

In the street, I turned left as instructed and followed the busy road. Before long, the university grounds were clearly in view about 300 metres ahead. Large expanses of lawn swept back from the street, buffering the buildings from the road.

Hundreds of students speckled the lawns, some in groups chatting, others solitary figures reading or asleep in the sun. I thought of my own days at university and felt a small thrill, an echo of that time, as I followed the path to the imposing stuccoed façade.

There was still 30 minutes until the session on the history of midwifery. A sign directed me to the Obstetrics Conference with an arrow pointing along a path to my left. At its end was a rust-red building attached to the central core of the university by a glassed artery. Double oak doors stood ajar, and I entered the foyer whose deep burgundy walls reminded me of a womb.

Several people were conversing on the landing at the rear of the entrance. A woman turned as I entered and came down to greet me. She smiled as we approached each other, and I was struck by the familiarity of her face.

"Buongiorno," she said, extending her hand in greeting. She was tall and thin, and her fair hair was swept back into a clasp above the roll neck of her black sweater. When she spoke her kohl-lined eyes were warm and expressive. She was not young, perhaps late forties, but she was beautiful. I scrutinised her, trying to jog my memory.

"I am Lucia Lorenzo," she said, as she took my hand.

Mentally I repeated her name, trying to find a connection. When I told her mine her eyebrows arched in surprise.

"Dottoressa Cavanagh."

"Have we met?" I said but was suddenly struck with the realisation that this was Lucia Lorenzo of the Fatebenefratelli Hospital. I scanned her face looking for proof that she was the woman in the Pantheon, the woman of my visions, but the idea seemed absurd.

She considered me. "No... we have not met, but I have heard of you."

Did she know about Bonnie's death, I wondered. Suddenly I felt like a sham and wished I hadn't come.

"I am very honoured that you attend from such a long way. When I saw your name on the attendance, I hoped that you might speak..."

"Oh, no..." Inwardly, I reeled at the thought. I had given many papers at conferences over the years, but it now seemed a lifetime ago and, momentarily, I struggled to remember the tenets of my own work.

She nodded in understanding and accompanied me to the landing.

"Registration this way," she said, and directed me with her elegant hand towards the doorway on the right. "Refreshments are available..."

I thanked her as she left me to join the others.

In the room she had indicated, I signed my name and scanned the extensive list for others I might recognise. Although practitioners of obstetrics were usually male, there were a large number of women enrolled in the conference. Given that the topic was midwifery, I was not surprised. In my years of practice, I had met only a handful of women who had trained to be obstetricians. Though numbers were increasing, it would take a long time for the gender imbalance to improve significantly.

Two show bags, one with my name, sat as lonely figures on the table. An announcement was directing people to the auditorium. The lecture theatre was a circular core in the ground floor of the building. It was an old design that didn't maximise space to an advantage. The central seating was near to capacity and there was a hum of enthusiastic greetings that was muted by the thick carpet. There were empty seats at the very front and I quickly descended the steps as the lights began to dim.

To respectful and appreciative applause, Lucia Lorenzo

took up her position at the podium. As the applause died, I heard the shuffling of a late entrant, the owner of the other bag, I assumed, a few seats behind me. As the introductory comments began, I silently rifled through the show bag for the program. Lucia Lorenzo was listed as chair of the conference and there was a short spiel beneath her photograph. I tilted the program towards the minimal light available. *"Dottoressa Lucia Lorenzo is head of obstetrics at the Fatenbenefratelli Hospital in Rome. As advisor to the Italian Government on women's health, she is a tireless proponent for increasing the role of trained women in the current practices of obstetrics and midwifery."*

I remembered that the receptionist had said that she was in England. I recalled how shocked I had been by her similarity to the woman in the Pantheon and, although in life she was older than in the photograph, the similarity was still obvious. Yet her interest in me didn't seem to extend beyond the professional. This woman's prominence in my imagination was just that, I concluded, my imagination.

Lucia Lorenzo spoke eloquently, her Italian inflections enhancing the listening value of her talk. Her introduction was an overview of the more recent history of the practices of obstetrics in the West. Slowly scrolling through images of the pioneers in the field that were projected on the whiteboard behind her, she occasionally paused to elaborate an individual's contribution. In the period up to the end of the 19th century, there were few women, but those who were represented had made significant contributions to our understanding and improvements in childbirth practices. I felt a sense of shame at my ignorance. She scrolled further back in time and away from America and Britain to Greece.

"The third century," she said, and paused. Though the image behind her was an artistic representation, the face that filled the screen was captivating. The artist had drawn the large, dark and determined eyes so that they followed the viewer. Above the full top lip was a faint shadow suggesting an indeterminate gender. The hair was hidden beneath the hood of a cloak though there was a sense of arrogance or forthrightness about the figure.

"Agnodice," Lucia said with pride and held the image on the screen. She told us the story of the Greek woman who trained to be an obstetrician. The story would be unremarkable if it wasn't for the fact that women were barred from studying. The significance of the shadow across the lip became clear. Agnodice had disguised herself as a man.

As I looked again into the eyes of Agnodice I was moved by her story as, it seemed, the artist had been. Over the next hour, I learned a great deal from Lucia Lorenzo. She was passionate about restoring obstetrics to what she saw was its rightful place to women. It was not that she dismissed the significant advances made by the men who came to dominate the profession, but she wanted to restore the feminine, to have acknowledged the ways of knowing that belonged to women.

When the image faded from the screen, she said: "Agnodice may not have existed at all. Anecdotes of her story have at their roots the customs and beliefs of the time but, my dear colleagues," and here she seemed to be addressing the women in the auditorium, "we are the living legacy of Agnodice and the women before us." She turned off the screen. "Tomorrow we will continue our history."

The room illuminated in stages and the audience began to rise with it. As the chatter died away into the corridor, I sat a while longer contemplating what I had learned and resolved to come back the following day. I'd thought everyone else had left but, as I collected my bag and notes there was a sound behind me and when I turned, I saw the back of a man disappearing through the rear door. There was no sign of him in the corridor or the foyer. Outside small cliques had formed as phone numbers and academic gossip were exchanged; for some reason, I doubted that he was among them.

I switched on my phone to check the time and was surprised to see that two hours had passed. The program offered a lecture on postpartum depression and, as I contemplated whether to go, the phone vibrated in my bag.

"Hi Dee." Madeleine's voice was bright, and I inwardly smiled at the sound of it.

"Hi Mads. Where are you?"

"Probably about... a mile away," she said, with exaggerated pomp. "We're at the Royal Crescent," she added with a hint of embarrassment. I knew the place and had eyed it lustfully on the drive into Bath.

"What's your plan?"

"Well, you've got lectures, haven't you?"

The program was still suspended in mid-air in my other hand. "Not until tomorrow."

"Oh ..." My sister's voice sounded surprised and there was a hint of something else.

"You've got something else to do?"

"Well, we had planned to head to Bristol for a few hours, but we can change..."

"It's OK, Mads, I've got a few things to do anyway. Will we meet for dinner?"

"Of course!" Her response was immediate and ineffective at hiding her relief.

We made a time and I offered to meet them at the hotel, a good opportunity to see the five-star-plus interior. With a few hours to kill, I reassessed the postpartum lecture but decided against it and wandered back along the path I had taken to the university.

At the road, I paused, wishing I'd had the foresight to bring a map and decided that the safest route was to return in the direction of my guesthouse. Traffic moved at a frenetic pace along the main roads into Bath and jarred my nerves more than it had ever done in Rome. When a side street became available, I turned into it, breathing a sigh of relief.

CHAPTER THIRTY-FOUR

In the quiet, my mind turned to Agnodice. Fact or fiction, she had affected me, though I wasn't sure how or why. Mentally, I searched Doctor Lorenzo's face again for its resemblance to my mystical woman. Although I could rationalise the similarities – fair hair, aquiline features would be common enough – I couldn't argue with the instinctive certainty that they were one and the same. But I didn't understand what it could mean. I acknowledged that perhaps something was tunnelling my vision. There was plenty of inner angst to tunnel it – Bonnie's death, Julian's departure, a career suspended in mid-air. If I probed deeper, I could find more – a checkered relationship with my mother, a fear of becoming barren as time went by and, when I admitted it, an envy of my sister's happiness. Yet none of these, felt like "it" and I wondered if, perhaps, there was nothing at all to explain it.

As a child, I had been a dreamer, inventing in my sleep wild and fantastic scenes that seemed to be made up of nothing more than insignificant images collected during the day. *Was it because now my mind was no longer busy with work and study that it was simply running free? Perhaps I was bored.* The thought gave me a sense of relief though I sensed some deeper part of me was not so easily convinced.

The side street opened into a large mall lined with shops. I wondered how the authentic British experience of Devonshire tea would compare with the one at Sophia's kitchen bench, but there seemed to be only chic, modern cafés. Resigning myself to a chai latte and organic muesli slice, I noticed, on the other side of the mall, a tearoom almost too quaint to be true. As I crossed over, I internally cringed. While my sister was "over the moon" with a famous Italian stud, I was choosing to spend solitary time with my head in the clouds of the grey and blue rinses that puffed behind the lace café curtain.

The door opened smoothly; no bell to welcome me as it had in Hyacinth's little shop. The coifs at the tables were not as cloudy as I'd thought but were impeccably combed. A woman, dressed in a black dress and crisp white apron approached me with a concerned look that suggested I'd stumbled into the wrong establishment. Though I guessed she was in her seventies, her impossibly black hair was parted down the middle and caught at the nape of her neck with a crimson bow. A Brontë fan, I thought, here in Austen country. I targeted her furrowed brow with a smile that disarmed her.

"Yes?" she said, forcing a smile.

"Tea and scones please," I said, aware that my Australian accent had puckered her lips.

One dyed eyebrow rose theatrically as she turned towards a table next to the refrigerated cabinet.

"I'd rather this one," I said, and sat down at a table by the window.

In barely time to boil a kettle, a pot of tea and bone-china cup were being placed before me. Two robust and perfectly glazed scones sat pertly on a plate surrounded by small dishes of strawberry jam and cream. I was surprised that I hadn't been given the runts of the litter. "Brontë" rested her pallid fingertips on the table briefly as if waiting for some type of response.

"They look beautiful," I felt compelled to say and restrained a chuckle.

She gave a soft snort and left to attend another table where, I noted, she gushed a blast of unseasonal warmth.

In a bracket on the wall were several different brochures and I picked out one on the sites of Bath. It detailed facts I already knew – the Georgian architecture, the Jane Austen connection, and the Roman Baths. I opened out to an annotated map of the famous historical site – the Great Bath and the East and West Baths. The King's Bath, I read, had been constructed at the site of the original sacred spring where the goddess Sulis Minerva had been worshipped in pre-Roman times. I felt as though my heart had stopped. I took a deep breath and read on: "According to legend, the Celtic King Bladud was cured of leprosy by the goddess of healing and fertility Sulis (or Sul), in the natural hot springs in 860 BCE. In the first century, the Romans built baths around the spring and a temple dedicated to Sul, and their own goddess, Minerva, and their adopted god, Asklepios..."

As I mentally spoke her name, I felt the pain begin as a small cramp in the pit of my abdomen. Slowly it spread in a wave through my pelvic floor, and I braced for the worsening, though it died away quickly. When I glanced up, my finger still pressed into the map, "Brontë" was eyeing me from above the swinging saloon doors that led to the kitchen. From the distance, her black hair and eyebrows gave her a malevolence that was heightened by the flame of the bow at her nape. When she disappeared into the kitchen, I placed the money under the napkin and left.

With the brochure tucked in my bag, I turned left into the mall and followed the signposts towards the Roman Baths. Although my body was weak, my senses were heightened as if electrified, though I was aware that my peripheral vision seemed dulled and grey. I knew that I should see a doctor, but, at my core, I felt calm and strong, and my pace suddenly quickened with the energy of a woman days before giving birth.

The street entrance to the baths was humble in comparison to the large foyer. A long queue had formed at the ticket box but there seemed to be equivalent numbers leaving. At the booth, an elderly man fumbled with the ticket dispenser.

"Tour?"

"No, thanks."

He handed me my ticket. "Sul awaits."

"Pardon?"

He smiled but then addressed the person behind in a gentle dismissal of me.

Further into the entrance, groups of tourists gathered around their guides like excited school children, and I wondered if I'd made the right decision to go it alone. I knew little detail about the history of the baths, but somehow, I felt that I was here for the present.

When the first tour group moved off, I tagged along behind at a discreet distance. On the terrace that overlooked the magnificent Great Bath, I learned that it was lined with lead sheets and that the encircling pillars would have supported an enclosing roof. From here, I followed the directions to a museum on the site of what was thought to have been a temple.

Inside, there were scores of people milling around the artifacts that were cordoned off in the centre of the building. Despite the crowd, the atmosphere was relatively quiet, and people talked in hushed tones as they stopped to inspect the various treasures. A gilded head of a goddess, larger than life, attracted the most attention. When I managed to get closer, I read that it was the bust of Sulis Minerva. I scrutinised the face, but the representation had no meaning for me.

At the rear of the building a broken section of a small marble altar was just visible through the crowd. I jostled closer to get a better view. A plaque named a figure of a man with outstretched arms as Apollo. Beneath his feet, a double line wove around the altar's base. At intervals, the space between the lines was crosshatched to represent the scales of a snake – Asklepios – and, as I followed its path at the back of the piece, I saw that it wound up and through the braided hair of another figure before coiling down into her open hand – Sulis Minerva. Beneath her feet, an inscription was crudely hacked into the rock. Its translation read simply: "Truth."

The pink tint in the marble, that I now recognised, gave an almost lifelike quality to the sculpture. Although the altar was fragmented and chipped, a small piece missing from Sul's palm caught my attention. On instinct I rifled through the internal pocket of my bag and brought out the packet that contained the stone. Discreetly, and disguising my moves with a tissue to my nose, I manouevred the stone in my fingers. I reached out and pressed it into the cavity in Sul's palm holding my breath in case an alarm should ring. At first it didn't fit, but I took it out and spun it around and tried again. It sat perfectly.

My hand retracted as if it had been scorched. Further down the room a security guard was watching. Frozen with anticipation, I waited for him to approach but he smiled and turned away. I looked back at the altar, doubting what had just happened, but Sul's palm was smooth. I couldn't distinguish where the stone had been inserted.

Stone steps worn with age and capped with rubber strips led to a passage on the lower level, the King's Bath. Here the air was sulphurous despite the vents cut into the rock. Ahead, reflected light danced on the walls in a repetitious code. My hand strayed to touch the wall next to me and I could feel the low hum of air conditioning reverberating somewhere above.

When I turned the corner around a worn and braced pillar, I held my breath. A pool of water large enough for 40 Romans was lit by submerged lights and, beneath the wispy clouds of steam, the water was green and surprisingly clear. At the opposite end of the chamber, a young couple was the tail end of a tour group and, behind me I could hear echoes of the next group approaching. I walked along the barrier, taking it in and read that this was the heart of the baths, built on the sacred spring where Sul had been worshipped long ago.

I sat on a recessed bench as a small group entered the chamber. They made sounds of wonder but passed to the other end where the guide gave them a potted history. Sul had brought me here. The thought caused an involuntary shiver down my spine to its base and spread, now in surges of pain, through my pelvis. I leaned back against the seat breathing deeply, aware that beads of sweat were forming rivulets down my abdomen. Five or six people passed but seemed to be unaware of my presence. I opened my mouth for help, but my throat was constricted and dry and my arms would not move.

Between muscular contractions I laid my head back against the seat and watched through hooded lids as the steam formed soft, cumulus clouds above the water. Animated bodies of women moved forward with outstretched arms. Fear and relief closed my eyes, and I gave my body into the gentle insistence of their hands. Between them I was lifted and placed on a rudimentary chair with back and arms constructed into the shape of pi. The seat had a crescent-shaped opening and was positioned beneath my perineum. Sweet and pungent-scented oils were rubbed into my breasts and abdomen and, as another intense contraction racked me, a wad of diluted vinegar was placed into the birth canal.

There were five women, dressed in simple robes and each had silver ribbon woven through her braided hair. They were familiar to me and when the pain subsided, I took in their faces —Ruth, Madeleine, Sophia, my mother and my aunt; they massaged my limbs and wiped my forehead when the next wave curled me out of the seat.

Across the waters of the spring a new body formed. Instantly I knew the aquiline nose, long fair hair. I called her name as she drifted forward and embraced me. The other women stepped aside for Sul to take her position on a small stool they had set in front of me. Together my five women sang sweet songs as they stroked my body. With one hand on my belly, Sul gently parted my thighs and, with her other, placed her fingers into my opening. A surge of pain, this time electrified and rolling, bore down through my pelvis and I writhed with pain, feeling as if my inside was being forced outward. Then, with a great heave, it was over. I closed my eyes and wept with joy – the pain already forgotten. When I looked again, Sul had gone, and the women were dissipating into the mist. Exhausted but exhilarated, I fell into a contented sleep.

CHAPTER THIRTY-FIVE

"Dee?" Gentle rocking woke me and when I opened my eyes the face was so close, I had trouble adjusting my vision. Madeleine was leaning over me, and I looked beside her for my mother, aunt, Ruth and Sophia.

"Dee," she said again in a small plea.

I wanted to answer but it was as if my body was still locked in a deep sleep. I wondered briefly if we were in Kos, or Rome. Was there a plane, a train to catch and I had overslept? At a deeper level, I knew this wasn't the case. I felt different, physically lighter as though I had shaken a heavy burden.

My eyes slowly adjusted to my sister's face. She was sitting back on the bed. When our eyes finally met, she smiled and gave a sigh that sounded like relief. I looked past her to take in the unfamiliarity of the room that was furnished more opulently than the others we had stayed in. There was a tall shadow in my right peripheral vision, and I turned my eyes to towards it. Carlo was leaning against the wall.

"Buongiorno, Dana," he whispered as he pushed off from

the wall and came to stand beside Madeleine. He, too, looked relieved and seemed to have physically changed since I'd last seen him. His face was less angular and sharp and there was a softness in his eyes. He rested a protective hand on Madeleine's shoulder and when she glanced up at him, I was able to envisage the many exchanges like this that would occur between them in the future. They were in love, and I felt genuinely happy for them for the first time.

The next day, so I have been told, I lay motionless in the bed and drifted in and out of a dreamless sleep. All that I remember was the feeling of a warm hand softly and gently stroking my forehead and the murmurings of a male voice. When the doctor came to re-examine me and to take blood samples, she stood by my bed looking perplexed. If I could have spoken, I would have told her that there was nothing wrong with me. I felt stronger than I could remember. I was healing from the inside out.

Whenever I woke, Madeleine was sitting beside me, and she would talk about trivial happenings of the day. She seemed to be alone at those times and busied herself adjusting my sheets and monitoring the amount of light in the room. On the third day, Carlo came in with Sophia. The sight of her stirred incredible emotion that was soothed by the stroke of her hand. As she and Madeleine looked down at me in the bed, I recalled my five women at the spring and their tender care. When Sophia leaned over me to speak, I looked into her eyes and saw a tannin-coloured pool in the shade of an oak tree. I smelled warm fruit offerings and saw Sul rise from the underworld. As she stepped on to the bank beneath the vast tree, the snake of Asklepios slithered from the waters and wrapped itself around her feet. Together they were beseeching me to do something.

When I turned to look behind me there were many people who had come to worship. Some were looking with fear at something on the ground. I went over to them and saw a woman in childbirth reaching out in pain; blood seeped down her thighs. Some threw charms beside her, but others turned away; children were in fear. Three women were standing near and I beseeched them to help me. As they stroked and calmed the woman, I parted her legs and felt for the baby's crown. Sing to her, I told them, and their sweet voices enveloped us. The woman's pelvis began its natural rhythm and into my hands a boy was born. When I had laid him on his mother's breast I turned towards the tree. Sul, and the serpent, had gone.

On the second day Madeleine placed the tray on my lap and plumped the pillows behind me. She sat on the bed and studied me while I sipped tea.

"What's the matter?" I said.

She seemed to be wrestling with something to tell me. "Nothing."

"Mads?"

"Well, we haven't talked yet about what happened to you."

I put down my cup and told her what I could remember, though I had little memory of it then beyond falling into a deep and restful sleep. She was silent and blank-faced as I spoke, nodding every now and then, but seemed to be holding something back.

"And so," I said, "we haven't spoken about how I came to be at your hotel."

She raised her eyebrows and let out a sigh as she leaned back.

"Dee... I'm not sure that you're well enough."

"Madeleine!"

She shifted her body on the bed, but her head was angled slightly away from me as though she was expecting a blow. "Julian found you."

My head jerked back into the pillows as though I was the one who had been slapped.

"Julian found me." The words made little sense to me.

"Yes," she said quietly and, I detected, guiltily. "He stayed with you in the ambulance on the way to the hospital, but you put up such a fight about not wanting to go there, they transferred you here instead."

There was so much she was telling me that I couldn't think where to begin, though at a deeper level I felt the shift of something coming into place.

"You told Julian I was in Bath?"

"Yes."

"Why?"

Madeleine coloured. "I was worried about you..."

"Where is he?"

She looked down at the bedcover, "In his room down the corridor. He's been here every day."

"In his room down the corridor." I replayed the words, trying to extract something solid and real in the syntax. Madeleine hadn't moved but was watching me carefully.

"He's been here every day?"

"Yes."

"How... is he?"

"Shattered."

"Why was he following me, Mads?"

She let out an exasperated laugh, "He's not following you. He loves you. He's been worried about you since the court case, calling me every day during that time... more if he had spoken to you earlier. Do you know he was there the day you were exonerated?"

"But why didn't he tell me?"

"You pushed him away, Dee. Julian never left you. You left him."

It was true. I knew it deeply. Another shift took place.

"It was Julian who sent the letters, wasn't it?"

Madeleine coloured. She studied the bedclothes waiting for my rebuke.

"He loves me," I said, instead.

She looked up. "Will I tell him to come in?"

Despite my longing to see him, I needed time to process all that had happened and all that I was hearing.

"No, not yet... I need time... to think."

Madeleine gave a small sigh of exasperation and raised her hand from her lap. She was holding something and moved it hesitantly towards me.

"What is it?"

"A letter... no, not one of the letters." She laughed but it had a nervous, anxious edge. It was handed in to reception, for you." Now my sister met my eye and held it. "I saw him, the one who left it. He's good looking, in a gigolo kind of way. Not your type."

I shifted my position a bit higher on the pillows and took the envelope from her hand, though she seemed reluctant to part with it. The front was simply addressed: "Dana." On the back was a single initial "E".

I slipped it under the sheet to read in a quiet moment. Madeleine seemed to be about to say something but thought better of it and, without a word, left me alone.

CHAPTER THIRTY-SIX

The next morning Sophia came again and sat by the bed embroidering a beautiful linen pillowslip.

"For Madeleina," she said, holding it up for my inspection. The centre was untouched, but around its perimeter were tiny flowers in red, blue and green. She resumed her stitching.

"Thank you," I said to the crown of her head.

She looked up.

"For coming."

She smiled. "Prego, Dana." Then she patted my hand.

While Sophia stitched, my thoughts turned to Julian. I wanted to see him, but I was still numbed and weary. I felt that I had changed, but I didn't know yet in what way.

"Sophia," I said to the peppered hair of her bent head. She looked up, but this time folded the pillowcase and laid it carefully on the bed. Taking my hand in both of hers she tilted her head to the side waiting for me to speak. I talked then, as I had at the villa, about Julian, that I loved him and always would, and I told her about Elliot. I said that I wanted to return to my work, that there would be a difference, that I would make a difference to the training of women in obstetrics and midwifery, but I didn't yet know how.

I listened to myself, surprised at what I was saying but knowing it was right. Sophia might not have understood but she nodded and stroked my hand; it was enough simply to be heard as layers of me shed. When I had finished, when I felt cleansed, she left and returned with a pot of lemon-balm-and-rosemary tea. Over the steam of our cups, she talked in her native tongue and, though I didn't know what she was saying, I understood that it was therapy, for both of us, simply to talk.

That night I dreamed I was in the Stourhead Pantheon. It was late spring, and fruit was budding within the vibrant green leaves of trees. The air that whirled lightly around my body was a mixture of warmth and of cold. The Abyssinian cat strolled out to greet me from beneath a nearby shrub. It wrapped itself around my legs and arched its back in anticipation of my stroke. The steps to the balcony merged with the tiers of the Asklepion and together we climbed as we had done in a past winter, though this time with youthful energy. At the door, we waited with joyful expectation. From the depths was the sound of footsteps ascending.

There was a pause, a slight creak as the door opened and, into the light, I stepped.

THE END

Dear reader,

We hope you enjoyed reading *A Single Breath*. Please take a moment to leave a review, even if it's a short one. Your opinion is important to us.

Discover more books by Amanda Apthorpe at https://www.nextchapter.pub/authors/amanda-apthorpe

Want to know when one of our books is free or discounted? Join the newsletter at http://eepurl.com/bqqB3H

Best regards,

Amanda Apthorpe and the Next Chapter Team

You might also like:

Hibernia by Amanda Apthorpe

To read the first chapter for free, please head to:
https://www.nextchapter.pub/books/hibernia

ACKNOWLEDGMENTS

I would like to thank Miika Hannila and the Next Chapter team for the incredible work on this republication; Helen Goltz for her expertise and support in its initial publication; and Marion M Campbell for her perceptive advice, encouragement and guidance throughout the writing and revision of this novel.

Most of all, I thank my partner Chris, my family and friends for their support and encouragement.

ABOUT THE AUTHOR

Amanda loves to write. No sooner has she inserted the final full stop on the latest novel and she's already shaping up for the next one. Amanda also loves to teach and to share with her students what she knows, and what she's still learning about writing. She holds a Master of Arts, and PhD in Creative Writing and is active in the national and international writing worlds, presenting at conferences and writing workshops.

A Single Breath accompanies *Whispers in the Wiring* on the actual and virtual bookshelves and *Hibernia* and *One Core Belief* are due for release soon. In addition to writing fiction, Amanda has two published volumes of the *Write This Way* series: 'Time Management for Writers' and 'Finding Your Writer's Voice', with more volumes on the way.

Amanda is a Melbourne (Australia)-based author, teacher and lifelong student of yoga.

Manufactured by Amazon.ca
Acheson, AB